DESPERADO

The girl was about sixteen, a long-legged, pale blonde in a blue cotton dress. She emerged from the house carrying a bucket. She walked to the garden plot and began watering the parched plants.

It was then the man emerged from the brush. He came up behind her. He grasped her waist with one hand. He cupped his other hand over her mouth and pulled her close to him so he could speak into her ear.

"Just do as I say and you won't get hurt."

The girl seemed to give in. Then she tried to break free. She almost made it. But the man managed to keep his grip on her.

The man's voice was rough now. "Nice try. But I've got a gun here. I won't hesitate to use it."

The man was Skye Fargo . . . in the tightest spot of his life . . . playing his most dangerous role . . . a man who everyone thought was a monstrous murderer . . . with his life riding on his trigger finger and a woman's trust. . . .

CHEYENNE CROSSFIRE

THE
TRAILSMAN
145

CHEYENNE
CROSSFIRE

by

Jon Sharpe

A SIGNET BOOK

SIGNET
Published by the Penguin Group
Penguin Books USA Inc., 375 Hudson Street,
New York, New York 10014, U.S.A.
Penguin Books Ltd, 27 Wrights Lane,
London W8 5TZ, England
Penguin Books Australia Ltd, Ringwood,
Victoria, Australia
Penguin Books Canada Ltd, 10 Alcorn Avenue,
Toronto, Ontario, Canada M4V 3B2
Penguin Books (N.Z.) Ltd, 182–190 Wairau Road,
Auckland 10, New Zealand

Penguin Books Ltd, Registered Offices:
Harmondsworth, Middlesex, England

First published by Signet,
an imprint of Dutton Signet,
a division of Penguin Books USA Inc.

First Printing, January, 1994
10 9 8 7 6 5 4 3 2 1

 REGISTERED TRADEMARK—MARCA REGISTRADA

The first chapter in this book originally appeared in *Abilene Ambush,*
the one hundred forty-fourth volume in this series.

Printed in the United States of America

The Trailsman

Beginnings . . . they bend the tree and they mark the man. Skye Fargo was born when he was eighteen. Terror was his midwife, vengeance his first cry. Killing spawned Skye Fargo, ruthless, cold-blooded murder. Out of the acrid smoke of gunpowder still hanging in the air, he rose, cried out a promise never forgotten.

The Trailsman they began to call him all across the West: searcher, scout, hunter, the man who could see where others only looked, his skills for hire but not his soul, the man who lived each day to the fullest, yet trailed each tomorrow. Skye Fargo, the Trailsman, and the seeker who could take the wildness of a land and the wanting of a woman and make them his own.

1860, Wyoming Territory—
where justice is swift,
and a man's life can hang on a thread of memory . . .
or at the end of a noose.

1

The pain pounded in heavy waves through his head. Skye Fargo lifted one hand to his forehead and rubbed it, coming slowly awake. He pulled the bedclothes up higher and turned onto his side. What had given him this headache? He stretched his limbs beneath the sheets and nuzzled the feather pillow. Maybe a little more sleep and the pain would go away, he thought dully. He inhaled and came fully alert at the unmistakable odor of blood, fresh and nearby.

Fargo sat bolt upright, his head whirling and pounding. Where the hell was he? He looked around.

He lay in a brass bed in a large white room well furnished with carved dark wood. The late morning light poured through the fluttering lace curtains.

Sprawled across the floor lay a woman in a white gown, facedown, her long dark hair tangled. A dark rivulet of blood snaked across the wide planks of the floor. There was no question she was dead—and had been for a few hours.

Fargo rubbed his head again and smelled blood. He slowly put his hand down and saw the blood on his hands had smeared the sheets of the bed.

Fargo gazed about the room again, confused. He didn't recognize it. Nothing, absolutely nothing was familiar to him. And his head hurt so much that thinking was painful. And who the hell was the dead woman?

Was it possible . . . ? His head reeled with the thought, and he quickly put it away, flinging aside the bedclothes and rising.

He was stark naked. Fargo quickly crossed to the washstand and rinsed the blood off his hands and arms. His clothes hung over the back of a nearby chair. He dressed hastily, fighting the waves of black pain that continued to roll from one ear to the other inside his brain. All the while, he looked down at the woman's body. He found his ankle holster on the chair, but the knife that went in it was nowhere to be seen. The Colt was in his holster, which he buckled around him.

This had to be a bad dream, Fargo told himself, but he knew it wasn't.

He knelt down beside the woman's body and gently turned her face up. She was pretty, dark brows against pale skin, a few freckles scattered across the bridge of her nose. Her cornflower blue eyes, still open, were blank. Fargo closed them. Blood was smeared across her cheek.

Her white lace nightgown had been slit down the front. She had been garrotted, stabbed in the chest numerous times, and then sliced open through the belly and her guts pulled out on the floor. Whoever had killed the woman had to have been a monster or have gone completely mad.

Fargo sat back on his heels, his mind racing, trying to remember—trying to remember anything about the girl, about the room. But he drew a blank. The memory was gone. Was it possible . . . ? He posed the question to himself again. Temporary insanity, madness? Was he capable of doing this? But even as he tried to imagine himself murdering the girl, he knew he didn't. And yet . . .

Fargo pulled the blanket from the bed and wound it around the girl's body. He bent down and lifted her in his arms. As he picked her up, he heard a clatter. His knife lay on the floor. Fargo carried her to the bed, laid her out, and covered her with a sheet.

The sound of a woman's voice from somewhere below him echoed down the hallway. He crossed the door and opened it slowly, just a crack, peering out. A short hall, a couple of chairs, and a table with a globe lamp was all there was to see. He closed the door silently. There was no lock so he pushed a chair under the knob. If someone, anyone, happened to come in, it would look for certain that he had murdered the girl. He needed time to figure out what had happened.

Fargo turned and surveyed the room. If he hadn't murdered the girl, then who had? And why was he being set up? And who was the girl, anyway?

Fargo looked her over again and then noticed a small opal ring on one of her fingers. With a silent apology to the dead girl, he took it off her finger and examined it. Inside was inscribed "HMK Always LJK." He pocketed the ring. If he ever found the girl's relatives, he'd return it. Meanwhile, it might be a clue to who she was and whatever had happened here.

Fargo searched the bureau and found only a silver brush and mirror, lingerie, and various lotions. Her dresses and coats hung in the closet. He looked for a purse or handbag, but there was none to be found.

On the writing desk were a pen and inkwell as well as a small supply of plain stationery and envelopes. He picked up the top sheet and held it flat so that the light would fall across it. Sometimes the pen nib made an impression on the second sheet and it could be read. No such luck. Fargo replaced the sheet of paper. He picked up the curved blotter and turned it over, hoping to find blotter paper with ink stains in the shape of a name or anything. But the blotter paper had been removed. Whoever had set him up had done a damn thorough job, Fargo thought to himself. With the exception of the ring, not a clue of the girl's identity remained.

Fargo crossed the window and looked out. The sloping tin roof glittered in the sun. Below he saw a quiet stable yard. Standing tethered to a fence just below was his Ovaro, and it was saddled. Fargo strained his memory again for anything, any shred of memory of the stable yard. Nothing.

He swore. It was all being set up just right, he thought grimly, his head still in agony. Here he was in the room with the girl. His knife had been used to murder her. His horse stood waiting for him to make a getaway. That was what they expected. That's what they wanted. Well, he thought, that's not what they would get.

And who the hell were *they*, anyway?

There wasn't time for another thought. A woman's light footsteps tapped hurriedly down the hall, pausing outside. The doorknob jiggled as she tried to open the door. The chair held. The doorknob jiggled again, impatiently.

Whoever it was stepped back from the door.

"Hannah?" the woman called. "Hannah? Are you all right?"

After a long moment she ran down the hall and called downstairs. Instantly Fargo heard the pounding of heavy feet running up the stairs.

"What's the matter?" a gruff voice called out. He heard other men's voices, at least four of them.

Fargo looked about. There was no escape, except by rolling down the roof and riding off on the Ovaro. But that's what they wanted him to do.

"The door!" the woman responded. "I can't get it open!"

"Stand back," one of the men shouted. A gunshot exploded the doorknob and latch, knocking the chair sideways. The door suddenly flew open and a huge man filled the door frame, his gun drawn. His dark red face was chiseled deep by lines like a streambed's rivulets. His eyes were cold black, his ebony hair snowy at the temples. A marshal's badge was on his leather vest.

"What the hell is going on in here?" the marshal shouted.

Fargo noted that he glanced first at the floor where the girl had lain and where her blood still darkened the wood. Then his eyes swept the room and saw the form under the sheet on the bed. Finally he locked eyes with Fargo who stood by the window.

"You murderer!" the marshal said.

Fargo's eyes narrowed.

"Why do you say that?" Fargo asked, his voice cool.

The huge man was taken aback and gaped for a moment. He took a step toward the bed and pulled back the sheet and blanket, revealing the girl in all her gore. The plump blond woman with a pug nose who had been standing right behind the marshal came inside the room after him. She spotted the murdered girl and shrieked. Three other men crowded in behind her and stood gawking.

"Murder!" she screamed. "Arrest him! Hang him!"

Fargo didn't move. He knew his life hung on how he reacted. Guilty men fled. Innocent men didn't. And he was innocent. With every passing moment he was more sure of it.

"I didn't kill her," Fargo said. "And I can prove it." The marshal stared back at him, his mouth open.

Fargo faced him down, his lake blue eyes cold, his chiseled jaw set and unyielding. He was bluffing. He couldn't prove his innocence but a bluff might buy him time. And time would bring him information and that might save his life.

"What . . . what do you mean you can prove it?" the marshal said. "You came into town last night. You got drunker and drunker. Then you came up here with Hannah. Of course you knifed her."

"How do you know it was a knife?" Fargo asked.

"I got eyes, don't I?" the marshal sneered. "She's cut up, ain't she?"

"Could have been a hatchet or a razor," Fargo said.

The marshal barked a laugh.

"He's crazy," the woman whispered so that everyone in the room could hear her. "Just shoot him."

The marshal exchanged looks with the woman and tightened the grip on his pistol.

As the shot exploded, Fargo dove sideways. The bullet grazed his shoulder as he drew the Colt and fired in one swift motion, aiming at the marshal's leg. His pistol clicked. Empty. Fargo shouted, enraged at his own stupidity as he hit the floor and rolled once. Of course they'd taken the bullets out of his gun.

A second shot whizzed by, barely missing him as he crashed against the wall and overturned the trash basket beneath the desk. In a flash Fargo saw his possible salvation. How could he have overlooked it? He reached out and grabbed the few papers in the basket, stuffing them into his shirt as he came to his feet. The marshal's pistol exploded again, catching him on the outside of the thigh, the impact hurling him against the wall. Fargo knew he'd been hit and bad. But he felt no pain. The pain would come later.

The marshal would kill him right here and now, Fargo realized. He'd have to do what they'd been wanting him to do all along—make a run for it.

Fargo bent his good leg and sprang headfirst through the window as a fourth shot shattered the air. His head and shoulders hit the glass, and it exploded outward, showering glittering shards. He rolled down the tin roof, over and over, holding his hands protectively across his face and eyes. The arrows of glass cut into his shoulders and back.

Fargo caught the edge of the roof and swung down, dropping to his feet. Another shot passed by overhead. The men shouted with fury at his escape. Or pretended fury, he thought.

Fargo took a few steps toward the pinto and mounted, pulling the reins toward him. The Ovaro whinnied and gathered its legs underneath it, vaulting over the rail fence of the yard and into a dusty street.

Fargo clung to the horse, hunching low as the bullets chased them down the street. He looked about, hoping to see something he recognized. The town, a few wooden buildings huddled together amidst some low buff hills, looked vaguely familiar—Wyoming Territory. Somehow he knew he was in Wyoming, but the rest was a blank. He headed straight down the street toward the edge of town and the wide open country beyond.

Now where the hell would they expect him to run? And how could he keep from going there?

The Ovaro galloped furiously as they passed beyond the last buildings. Fargo turned in the saddle to see if he was being pursued.

WELCOME TO BENTWOOD, he read on the sign pointing into town. He could see the men running out into the main street toward their tethered horses to pursue him.

He turned in the saddle again as the road took a turn and carried him out of sight. He had no doubt another bunch of men was waiting for him somewhere just ahead. His keen eyes scanned the barren

16

hills. He would be trapped between the two groups of men, and they would drive him into some deserted spot and shoot him or hang him—or both.

And it wouldn't matter what he said or what was the truth. They'd be certain they had found the murderer. And that would be justice enough.

Fargo scanned the hills again, lost in thought. The marshal and the men following were counting on the fact that Fargo would be trying to put many miles between him and Bentwood right now. The ambush was sure to be just ahead, close enough that he would run into it in the first wave of panic. Fargo smiled for the first time all day. That was exactly what he wasn't going to do.

Fargo brought the pinto to a halt and turned it off the road. They plunged down into a sage-choked ravine, out of sight. He dismounted and inspected his thigh. The bullet was imbedded in the muscle toward the outside. He'd been damn lucky. It hadn't shattered the bone or severed his artery, in which case he'd have bled to death in minutes. But the ugly wound was seeping and starting to throb like hell. And the leg hung useless. Whatever he did, he had to have the bullet pulled out right away, but he doubted he could do it himself.

Approaching hoofbeats sounded on the road. Fargo peered out of the thicket as the marshal and the three men swept by in a cloud of dust. He had only a matter of minutes before they discovered he wasn't ahead of them, and they turned back to look. Fargo swung up on the horse. He was beginning to feel the leg now. It wouldn't be long before the pain would be intolerable.

He needed to get somewhere safe soon. There was no chance he could face down the men. Fargo didn't even bother to look in his saddlebag since he was sure that whoever had unloaded the Colt had also taken his extra bullets.

The safest place right now was the last place they would look for him, in the middle of the town of Bentwood. Fargo kept the pinto walking through the underbrush beside the road for the short distance back to Bentwood.

Near a stand of dead cottonwood at the edge of town, he slid down. He removed the saddle and bridle from the pinto and hid them in the thicket. He stroked the pinto and the faithful Ovaro nuzzled him. The horse's distinctive black and white markings would be a dead giveaway if it was spotted tethered in town. The pinto would be safer running free. And if he needed it, he would whistle. The horse, if it could hear him, would come.

If he got caught, he'd be damned if he wanted the proud and free Ovaro to end up the stolen property of the marshal or his men. No, the horse was better running free.

"Get on out there," Fargo said quietly to the pinto, slapping its withers gently.

The Ovaro snorted uneasily and took a step, then turned to look back.

"Get," Fargo said again. The Ovaro started out toward the open land reluctantly, turning from time to time to look back at Fargo.

This side of the town seemed quiet, Fargo noted, turning away from the pinto. He'd need a hell of a lot of luck if he was going to stay alive for the next few hours. And luck seemed in short supply on this particular day.

Fargo encircled the town, watching carefully, keeping under cover of the scrub. At the back of one building was a dusty yard. A big yellow dog dozed in the shade, and a small garden plot withered under the sun's glare. Just then a young slender girl in a blue cotton dress emerged from the house, carrying a bucket. Sunburnt with pale blond hair and long, doe-like legs, she seemed to be about sixteen. She walked quickly toward the garden plot and began to pour water carefully on the dispirited plants. She stood facing the house with her back toward Fargo.

This was his chance. It was damned hard to move quickly and silently, dragging one leg behind him, but in a moment Fargo emerged from the brush and came up behind her. He grasped her suddenly, noting the curved slenderness of her waist. He cupped his other hand over her mouth and pulled her close to him so that he could speak into her ear.

"Just do as I say and you won't get hurt."

She dropped the bucket and struggled in his grasp, trying to bite his hand.

"Easy," he said. "Walk with me to the house. Or else."

The girl continued to struggle for a moment as he held her tight. Then she seemed to give in. She took a step or two toward the house, but stumbled, pitching forward. Fargo, his wounded leg exploding pain at every step, lost his balance, and the two of them tumbled to the ground, rolling over.

Fargo managed to keep his hand on the girl's mouth and his grip on her waist. He staggered to his feet, jerking her roughly. His leg screamed in protest.

"Nice try," he said in her ear, his voice gruff with the pain. "But I've got a gun here. I won't hesitate to use it."

Fargo hated to terrorize the girl, but he doubted she'd ever believe his story. His only chance was to play the role of a murderer on the run, desperate enough to kill anyone who got in his way.

The spirit seemed to go out of the girl, and she moved toward the building without another incident. The yellow dog awoke and looked up dolefully as they passed by, but didn't rise or growl. They climbed up the short stairway and Fargo pushed her ahead past the door.

Fargo glanced about. They stood alone in a kitchen with a stove and a wooden counter. In the corner stood an old table with two mismatched chairs, set with two plates and mugs. Ragged curtains hung at the window. Everything was clean, but he could tell the girl and her family didn't have much money.

"I'm about to take my hand away from your mouth," he said quietly. He drew his pistol, still holding her close with his arm. He jammed the barrel of the Colt just under her ribs and cocked the hammer for effect.

"One word from you and . . . Remember what I said," he whispered. It didn't matter that the Colt was empty now, Fargo thought to himself. He wouldn't shoot the girl even if she called out. But she didn't know that.

She nodded, trembling. Fargo slowly took his hand away.

"Who else is at home?' he whispered. "And keep your voice down."

"Nobody," she said. "We're alone."

Fargo jerked her hard against him, and she cried out.

"Don't lie to me," he warned her. He had an instinct that someone else was in the house.

"Francine?" a woman's voice called from above.

The girl hesitated.

"Answer her," Fargo said. "Keep it normal. If you tip her off, I'll shoot her."

"Yes, Mother?" Francine called out, trembling.

"I thought I heard you call," the voice said, concerned.

"No. No, everything's . . . fine."

"Very good," Fargo said. "Now ask her to come down and help you with something."

"I can't," Francine whispered. "She's sick. She hasn't been out of bed since spring."

"That's better," Fargo said. He could tell she wasn't lying. "You keep telling me the truth, and everything will be just fine. Anybody else at home?"

Francine shook her head no.

"Let's go up," Fargo said.

She led the way through the small rooms, furnished sparsely and poorly, although everything was well-kept and clean. They climbed the steep stairs awkwardly, Fargo leaning heavily on her, favoring his good leg. The bullet wound was excruciatingly painful now. He ground his teeth as they climbed.

At the top of the stairs he halted and put a hand out to steady himself until the waves of pain subsided somewhat and he could go on.

"Francine?" the mother's voice called again. "Is that you?"

"I'm . . . coming," the girl said.

They entered a small room with sloping ceilings and an iron bed. On it lay a pale woman, her auburn hair pulled back from her tired face. Her eyes widened and she sat up weakly as her daughter and Fargo entered the room.

"Oh, my God," the woman said. She clasped her hands in front of her. "Please, sir. Please. Do anything you like with me, but please leave my daughter alone. Please, I beg you."

Fargo pushed Francine down on a chair and leaned against the wall. He chewed the inside of his lip to keep the room from whirling crazily around him as the pain radiated up his leg. He noticed the women looking at his torn thigh, which he knew without looking had bled all the way down his Levi's.

Fargo released the hammer of his Colt and cocked it again, looking over the two women.

"Anybody else in the house?" Fargo asked the sick woman.

She shook her head.

"What's your name?" He pointed the barrel toward the bedridden woman.

"Marilyn Foster," she murmured. Her eyes were wide with fear. Francine slid from her seat and went to sit beside her mother on the bed. The two women held hands as Fargo watched them for a moment.

"Who else lives here?" he asked.

"No one," Francine said quickly.

Fargo pointed the Colt and adjusted his finger along the trigger.

"There were two plates on the table downstairs. And Marilyn doesn't get out of bed. Who else lives here?"

"Tommy," Francine said, her face pale.

"He'll be home from school any moment," Marilyn put in.

"He's my husband," Francine said. "He . . . teaches school. He's big and he's got a gun. And when he walks in, I'll scream and he'll kill you."

"Nice try," Fargo said. "No wedding ring?"

Francine looked down at her naked fingers and blushed, biting her lip.

Just then a door slammed downstairs, and Fargo heard the sound of running feet.

"Ma! Francie! I'm home!" The voice was that of a young boy.

"Shut the door," Fargo said to Francine. "And do exactly as I say. Otherwise, I'll shoot the kid right between the eyes." He kept his voice low and menacing.

Francine rose and closed the door just as Tommy's footsteps could be heard climbing the stairs.

"Hold it shut," Fargo said, moving beside her so he could whisper his instructions to her.

"Tell him your mother's had a bad attack. Real bad. He can't come in. And to fetch the doctor. Quick. Or else she might die. Got it?"

Francine did as she was told, shouting the instructions to Tommy on the other side of the door.

"Ma? Ma?" Tommy called, his voice scared. "Just hold on, Ma. I'll be right back with the doc!"

Tommy ran down the stairs and out the door, slamming it behind him. Everything was silent for a long moment.

"Good," Fargo said. He pushed Francine toward Marilyn's bed. "Sit over there where I can keep an eye on you both. Now we wait."

Fargo pulled a chair toward him and sank down on it. A thousand Indians were now hatcheting his leg, tearing into it in a thousand painful places and setting fire to his flesh. Once again he fought the waves of blackness that threatened to drown him.

"How long you been in Bentwood?" Fargo asked the women suddenly. He need to talk, to keep his mind moving so he wouldn't black out.

"A year," Marilyn said, bitterness in her voice. "Came from Missouri, just in time for the influenza epidemic."

"That what you got?" Fargo asked the sick woman. She shook her head no.

"It killed my dad," Francine said shortly.

Fargo nodded slowly, imagining the two women trying to get by in the rough town without a man in the house. He felt himself relax by slow degrees. He fought it and then holstered his Colt. He could draw it in an instant and wave it about again, if needed.

"You're the one who murdered that girl, aren't you?" Marilyn asked nervously.

Fargo looked at her with narrowed eyes.

"What are you talking about?" he said slowly.

"That girl at the Dusty Rose Saloon . . . " Marilyn's

voice trailed off, and her face grew even paler, frightened of his reaction.

"What do you know about that?" Fargo asked, anger in his voice.

Marilyn shrugged.

"I said, what do you know?" Fargo repeated, resting his hand on the butt of the holstered Colt.

"Just what I read in the paper," Marilyn said hastily. She handed a folded newspaper to Francine, who hesitantly rose and handed it to Fargo.

Fargo unfolded the newspaper. There on the front page were screaming headlines: DUSTY ROSE DAME DEAD, BRUTAL BUTCHER ON THE LOOSE.

Goddamn it. It had been just over an hour since the marshal and his cronies had burst in on him and the dead girl. And here he was on the front page of the morning newspaper. It didn't make sense. Once again Fargo wondered when he'd wake up from this nightmare.

He glanced at the story, but couldn't read it because the hatchets were hacking again at his thigh and dark undulations clouded his vision, causing the letters of newsprint to jump all over the page. But one thing he couldn't miss. There in the center of the front page was a drawing of his face, not a very good one. But the dark beard and hair, the deep eyes and strong jaw were unmistakably his.

And underneath was written: $500 REWARD FOR INFORMATION. $2000 DEAD OR ALIVE.

Oh yeah, Fargo thought. He'd been set up, and set up good.

with ruled off-anjie hat. Her eyes would have curled of his worlds.

"But the boy knew about that," Fargo raised his eyes to her.

"Well, with an ounce of luck there'd have been no harm to the mind of a Remington.

But with a flick of his knife, Mr. Well with. hat a little twist of the wrist - a Marine's closed morn remained behind it in fear.

2

Fargo ground his teeth as he held onto consciousness. The room and the pale frightened faces of the two women before him swam with exploding stars and black waves. If he passed out, he knew he was done for.

Just then he heard the door open below and voices. The doctor had arrived, brought by the boy. Fargo rose and limped to the bedroom door, positioning himself behind it, Colt in hand. He signaled to the two women to stay where they were on the bed. In another moment the door opened.

"Marilyn!" the man's voice said, concerned.

"Thank you for coming, Doc Blair," the woman answered, despair and apology in her voice.

"Ma!" The boy ran toward the bed. "Are you all right?"

Fargo slammed the door behind them.

Doc Blair, a pudgy man with silver thinning hair, spun about at the sound. His face registered shock, then immediate comprehension as he spotted Fargo's blood-soaked thigh. His hand tightened on the handle of his black leather bag, but otherwise he made no move.

"Who are you?" Tommy asked defensively, standing protectively by his mother and sister. His voice quavered, but he was trying to be brave.

"The man from the Dusty Rose," the doctor said, half to himself.

"You read the paper, too?" Fargo asked, nodding toward the newspaper with his face plastered across the front.

"No need to," Doc Blair answered. "They're putting up wanted posters with your picture on it all over town. By this afternoon they'll be all over the territory. They're calling you The Butcher."

Fargo swore. It was inconceivable that they could have printed wanted posters in the hour since they found him in the room with the dead girl. Whoever had set him up had been ready with all the pieces before Fargo had even awakened in the room.

He glanced at his four hostages. At some point they might start giving him trouble. He'd have to keep them off balance and still get the goddamn bullet out of his leg.

"You got some coffee made up?" he asked Francine.

"A whole pot of it on the stove," she said eagerly. "I'll . . . go downstairs and heat it up for you." Her voice betrayed her, and Fargo knew she would try something—call for help or attempt escape.

"Come here," he said.

She rose from the bed and approached the door. He grabbed her around the waist again and put the barrel of the Colt to her neck. She stiffened, and her mother gasped.

"Okay, Tommy," Fargo said. "Get downstairs and bring up that pot of coffee. Don't bother heating it. And fetch that coil of rope I saw hanging by the back door. If you're not up here in one minute, your sister is dead. Got it?"

The boy rose and dashed from the room. Fargo felt sorry for the kid. He hated to scare them all, but he knew it was his only chance for survival. Tommy was back in a moment.

Fargo released Francine and shoved her toward the bed. All the while, Doc Blair had not taken his eyes off Fargo. His gaze was penetrating, perceptive.

"Okay," Fargo said. "Tommy, stand over there. If everybody does what I say, nobody is going to get hurt. Now, Doc. I want you to tie up these women tight—to the bed."

The doctor nodded. Fargo drew the knife from his ankle holster. Marilyn, lying on the bed, stifled a cry. Fargo realized that the newspaper story must have told how the girl had been cut up. Fargo instructed Tommy to hold the rope. Fargo cut it into pieces so the doctor could secure the women.

"I'm going to check those ropes, so make them tight," Fargo told the doctor. Even from across the room Fargo could tell the doc was following his instructions. After the two women were tied up, Fargo told the doctor to stand back and, keeping him covered with the Colt, Fargo tested the ropes.

Suddenly a scream of rage came from Tommy, and the boy flung himself toward Fargo, pounding with his small fists against Fargo's back. Fargo whipped about, reached out, and held the struggling boy at arm's length. The doctor stepped forward, and Fargo pointed the Colt at him. He froze.

"You're a brave kid," Fargo said as Tommy flashed him a look of pure hatred. "If I were you, I'd do the same thing. But behave yourself, and I promise I won't hurt your sister and your mother."

Tommy slowly subsided and blinked back tears of frustration. "Go sit over there," Fargo said, pushing him toward his mother. Fargo limped to the door, dragging a chair with him. He closed the door and positioned the chair against it. Then he sat down.

"Bring me that coffee and put a chair under this bad leg," he instructed the doctor. "And let's get this bullet out."

Doctor Blair did as he was instructed. Then he cut open the leg of Fargo's Levi's, peeling the denim back from the ragged edges of the wound. He reached for his scalpel and a towel to stanch the bleeding.

"I've got a bottle of morphine," the doc said.

Fargo looked at him hesitantly. Yes, the opiate would dull the pain. But it would also dull his reactions, making him groggy. He shook his head no. The doc raised his eyebrows quizzically and lowered the scalpel toward the wound.

Digging out the bullet hurt like hell. Fargo found himself wishing for a good swig of whiskey. But whiskey would put him to sleep. And he had to stay awake. So he drained the coffee from the pot while the doctor cut and probed. Blood dripped onto the floor. White hot agony roared along his leg as his exposed bloody muscles were sliced or pushed aside in the search for the lead slug. The damn thing about a bullet wound was that sometimes you got more damage getting the thing out. Fargo concentrated on keeping his Colt trained on the doctor as he worked. As he fought off the pain, Fargo silently swore every curse he could think of and then made up some new ones.

"You were damned lucky," the doc said at last, holding the lead slug in the tongs. "A few inches to the other side and you'd be crippled or dead."

Fargo nodded, not trusting himself to answer. His jaw was so clenched he wasn't sure he could release it. During the entire operation he had not uttered a sound. And even though it had been agonizing, Fargo had seen enough of the operation to know that Doc Blair had done a damned good job. A less expert doctor would have taken longer and made him suffer more.

"A couple of stitches and that's it," Doc Blair said, threading his needle. "You've lost a lot of blood though, so you ought to . . . to rest."

Fargo smiled bitterly and stretched his jaw.

"Not likely," he rasped.

The doc nodded and bent over the leg, stitching it expertly. When he had finished, he bandaged the thigh neatly and began washing up with water from a pitcher on the night table.

Fargo sat in a chair positioned against the door, his leg propped on the chair before him. He felt exhaustion overtake him. His body screamed for sleep, but he ignored it.

"You were a helluva quiet patient," the doc said

with awe in his voice as he dried his hands on a towel. "I've heard tough men scream themselves hoarse with a wound like that. And they were liquored up. You didn't make a sound." The doctor looked at him for a long moment. "Who are you anyway?"

"Name's Fargo. Skye Fargo."

The doctor's face registered shock.

"Skye Fargo?" Marilyn said from the bed, her wide gray eyes staring. "You?"

"He can't be," Tommy said. "He's lying. Skye Fargo is a good guy."

"Back in Missouri we heard a lot of stories about you," Marilyn said. "You were my husband's hero. Tommy's too. Tom, my husband, always wanted to meet you. Now I'm glad he didn't."

I guess the stories were wrong, Ma," Francine said. "It turns out Skye Fargo is just a low-down murderer."

"I didn't do it," Fargo said simply. The time for pretense was over. "I didn't kill the girl. I woke up this morning in the room with her body. It was a setup."

"Sure," Francine said. "Sure, that's what they all say."

"Who set you up?" the doctor asked. He continued to gaze piercingly at Fargo as if trying to read him.

"That's the damdest thing," Fargo said. "I'm having a hard time remembering how I got here. I can't remember anything about this town or last night."

"Hmph," Doc Blair said. He hung the towel on a hook and approached. Fargo tightened his grip on the pistol.

"No," the doc said. "I just want to look at your eyes." He peered into Fargo's eyes searchingly, from one to the other. "Just as I thought. I need to feel the back of your head."

Fargo nodded, but kept his grip on the Colt. The doctor's fingers searched his scalp thoroughly and expertly, probing and pressing. It hurt and Fargo winced. Finally the doc took his hands away.

"Head trauma," Doc Blair said. "Your eyes don't match up. One of your pupils is a lot bigger than the other. You've had a bad blow to the head. Some blunt instrument because there's no break in the skin. But there is internal bleeding inside your skull. You've got amnesia."

"Amnesia," Fargo said. "Forgetfulness. But I remember my name and what I was doing last week."

"Yep," the doc said. "But you don't remember the events leading up to the moment of injury. That's typical."

"Terrific," Fargo said, his voice sharp. "That's just great." He subsided into an angry silence. Hell, he'd been knocked out a lot of times before and never had amnesia. And the one time he needed his memory to save his life, he couldn't remember anything. The doctor was watching him closely, as if reading his thoughts on his face.

"I suggest you try to rest for a few hours," the doc said. "The amnesia from a head blow is usually temporary. You could start remembering in a few days— weeks at the most."

"I don't have a few days," Fargo said.

Doc Blair nodded grimly. He picked up his instruments and began packing his bag.

"Who knows you're here?" Fargo asked the doctor.

"No one," Doc Blair said, pausing as he fitted the steel instruments into the leather loops inside his bag. "I was alone in my office when Tommy came to fetch me."

"And your wife?"

"I'm a widower."

"You understand I can't let you leave here? I can't take the risk," Fargo said, exhaustion in his voice. Despite the pot of coffee he drank, his body, his leg, and his head called out for sleep more than anything.

"I thought that might be the case," Doc Blair answered, closing his black bag.

"You can't keep us tied up forever," Francine said. Her face was a picture of confusion, anger, and fear.

"No. But right now I need some rest. And then, when it's dark, I'll try to get out of town." Fargo wasn't certain what his next step would be. But he realized he was too sleepy to think about it clearly.

Fargo instructed Tommy to tie the doc in a chair. The boy did as he was told. Fargo attempted to rise in order to check on the bonds, but his leg was throbbing, and the effort was beyond him. He made Tommy lie down on the floor in front of him, resting his head on a pillow from the bed. Fargo propped his good leg on the boy so that he would awaken instantly if the boy moved. Then he folded his arms across his chest, clutching the Colt as he leaned the chair against the door and closed his eyes.

"I . . . just need an hour or two of . . . sleep," Fargo

heard his voice saying. The blackness welled up to engulf him, and his last thought was a fervent hope that he would wake up and find it had all been a dream.

Fargo came awake to find Doc Blair bending over the bed, untying Marilyn. Clearly Tommy had not tied the doc very tight. He half-closed his eyes and listened to them whisper. The boy lay still on the floor, breathing softly in sleep.

"I think we should try to get away," Francine was whispering.

"No, no," the doc responded. "Just do as he says."

"But . . . he killed that girl," Marilyn whispered. "Do you believe he's innocent?"

"He's not a killer," the doc said. "I've seen killers and he's not one."

Fargo decided to let them know he was awake. He groaned and stretched and opened his eyes. The doc was standing by the bed, his hands raised in the air.

"Marilyn and Francine were getting cramps," Doc Blair said apologetically. "We weren't trying to escape. Honest."

"I believe you," Fargo said. He raised his foot from the sleeping boy. Tommy started and awoke. His eyes opened, and he saw Fargo. His face showed fear as he remembered.

Fargo glanced out the window. A few of the rooftops of the town of Bentwood were visible. Above, the scattered clouds in the clear blue sky were lit gold and ruddy by the setting sun. In another hour it would be fully dark and time to move. But where?

His leg was throbbing painfully, but he knew it was just a matter of time before the pain subsided. A day, maybe two. Then it would be stiff for a long time. Fargo realized he was very hungry and hadn't eaten all day.

"Let's go downstairs and get some supper," he said. "Then I'll head out and leave you in peace."

Fargo instructed Doc Blair to carry Marilyn in his arms, while he followed them, leaning on Francine and covering them with his empty Colt. Tommy led the way down the steep stairs. When they reached the kitchen, Fargo sat heavily in one of the chairs and Marilyn in the other, drawing her shawl around her nightdress. She was a pretty woman, with abundant auburn hair and wide gray eyes above catlike high cheekbones. He felt sorry again for the difficult life she must be leading.

At Fargo's orders the doc locked the back door, closed the curtains tight, and brought more chairs into the kitchen. Francine fried up steak and potatoes and made another pot of coffee. They ate in silence and then pushed back from the table, enjoying the coffee.

"Are all those stories true about you, Fargo?" Doc Blair asked.

"Most of 'em," Fargo answered.

Tommy drank a glass of milk, his eyes wide and riveted on Fargo.

"You've lived and loved enough for a hundred men," the doc said.

"Yep," Fargo agreed. "I'd like to make it a hundred and one. Only trouble is, I can't remember anything.

Just woke up this morning in a strange room with a dead girl. Then the marshal busted in with his men."

"Marshal Pike?" the doc asked. Fargo shrugged. "Big guy with bushy brows and black hair?" Fargo nodded.

Fargo leaned back and took a sip of the coffee, accidently spilling it down the front of his shirt. He wiped his hand against the cotton fabric and felt paper rustling against his skin. He had completely forgotten about the papers he had grabbed from the dead girl's wastepaper basket. He drew them out.

"I found these in the room," he explained. "Maybe they'll tell me who really killed the girl."

Fargo examined each of the pieces of paper as he uncrumpled them and flattened them on the table before him.

The first was a bill from a dressmaker made out to H. M. Kempner and dated two days before. He noted the name of the shop and set it aside. Marilyn reached for it excitedly and read it, handing it to her daughter. The second piece of paper was torn in half. It was the beginning of a letter, but some words were crossed out as though it was a draft. Fargo read it aloud.

"Dearest Lillian," it read. "Regarding what I wrote you in our last letter, I am now completely certain. You are the only one who can help me. Here is the proof. When I meet you, we will take it to . . . " There the letter ended where it had been torn. Fargo swore and turned the letter over, finding nothing on the back.

He uncrumpled another wad of paper; it read: "2 and 6. The Golden Room." The six was underlined. Fargo laid the paper aside.

The next piece of paper was the continuation of the letter. " . . . the man I told you about. He will know what to do with it. I have heard he is in Cheyenne or thereabouts. I'll see you soon, dearest sister. Hannah."

There were two other pieces of blank paper and a soap wrapper. That was all. Fargo sat back, lost in thought.

"So, the girl knew something," Doc Blair said. "Something she had proof about. And that got her killed."

"She sent something to her sister," Marilyn put in.

"Whose name is Lillian Kempner," Fargo said. "I wonder if Hannah got this letter to Lillian before . . . " He fished in his shirt pocket and brought out the small opal ring he had taken from the dead girl's finger. "Look at the initials inside." He passed the ring to Doc Blair. Tommy held out his hand to see the ring, too.

"Same initials," Fargo continued. "Maybe Lillian gave this ring to Hannah."

"So, I guess the first thing is to figure out what that 'proof' was?" Marilyn said. The color was back in her cheeks, Fargo noted—probably from all the excitement. She suddenly looked lovely and alive, so different from the pale drawn woman who had been in the bed.

"No," Fargo said. "Hannah knew she was being watched. So she was careful about leaving no clues. I doubt we'd ever figure it out, unless we knew what she knew. The more immediate question is how do we find the sister? If that letter was delivered, then Lillian is in as much danger as Hannah was."

"This is horrible. Horrible," Marilyn said despairingly.

"What do you suppose this means?" Fargo asked, pointing to the small slip of paper. Doc Blair looked thoughtful for a moment.

"Well, the Golden Room is a new saloon in Cheyenne." The doc thought for another moment. "Wait! Two and six! Those are the times the regular stagecoach arrives in Cheyenne on Saturdays!"

"The six is underlined. I'd guess that the sister of Hannah, Lillian Kempner, is coming in on the six o'clock stagecoach on Saturday," Fargo said. "How far are we from Cheyenne?"

"A hundred or so miles," the doc answered. "You got only six days. And you can't ride with that leg. It will tear apart and start bleeding again."

"I'll take the chance," Fargo said. "My life depends on finding out what Hannah knew. And if I don't get to Lillian before those others do, she might die as well. She can save my life, and I can save hers. I have to go."

Doc Blair opened his mouth to answer, but just then they heard men's voices in the yard outside. All of them froze. The voices spoke a few low words, and then heavy footsteps climbed the steps at the back door. A loud knock resounded through the stillness.

"Anybody home? Open up. It's Marshal Pike. Open up!"

3

Fargo glanced at Marilyn's wide gray eyes. One word from her, he knew, and he'd be caught. Marilyn Foster looked at him for a long moment, searchingly, as she made up her mind. then she pointed wordlessly to a narrow closet just behind him. She wanted him to hide inside of it. He silently rose. From the look of the small closet door, he doubted he would fit inside, but once he opened it, he found he could just squeeze inside with the brooms and dust rags. It was a perfect hiding place, where they'd not bother to look.

"Just a moment!" Marilyn's voice called out to the marshal. He heard the sound of chairs moving and someone's footsteps—probably Francine's—running upstairs. Fargo suppressed a sneeze as the dust from the rags tickled his nose.

"Marshal Pike!" Doc Blair's voice said as he unlocked the door. "Come right in."

Heavy boots clomped across the floor.

"What are you doing here, Doc?" Pike's gruff voice asked.

"Looking in on Marilyn," Doc answered. "She's

seems to be doing better. Much better. See, she's even up out of bed."

"We're looking for that butcher that cut up the girl over at the Dusty Rose," the marshal said. "She was slit all the way up the front of her and her guts got pulled out all over the floor." The marshal seemed to enjoy retelling the gruesome details. "He's a big, tall man, dark beard and hair. You seen him?"

All it would take would be a single gesture toward the closet where he was hiding, and it would all be over, Fargo thought in a flash. Marshal Pike and his men would shoot and shoot to kill. He knew that Marilyn and her family needed the money and needed it bad. But there wasn't a moment of hesitation when Marilyn answered.

"No, Marshal. My daughter's upstairs at the moment. We haven't seen any strangers all day."

"I'll have to search the house," the marshal said. The men moved off.

"Ma, what'll happen if they find him?" Fargo heard Tommy whisper.

"What was that?" the marshal's voice boomed, suspicion in every word. He had clearly overheard Tommy's remark.

"My son was asking what you'll do with that butcher when you find him," Marilyn answered evenly. "They'll hang him, honey," she said to Tommy. "Just like he deserves." She was a cool one, Fargo thought.

"Yeah, we'll string him up all right," the marshal said. Fargo heard the lingering suspicion still in his words.

In a few minutes the men reassembled in the kitchen.

"Well, keep your doors locked and your eyes open," the marshal said. "We don't know how far away this butcher has gotten. In another hour we'll have finished searching every house in town. He's dangerous, and he's got a particular taste for young pretty ladies like you."

Fargo knew this last remark was aimed right at Marilyn. The marshal and his men left the house. He heard them moving toward the next house. Fargo did not move.

"Sit down and continue like normal," Fargo said in a low voice from inside the closet. "They'll be back in a minute."

Francine's footsteps entered the kitchen a moment later. She stopped dead.

"Where's Skye? What's—?" She sounded stricken and worried for him, Fargo noted.

"Sit down here," Doc Blair interrupted sternly. "Better yet, you got some pie?"

"Sure, apple," Francine said. "But, did they—?"

"Then serve it up, girl!" the doc almost shouted at her.

The four of them ate in tense silence while Fargo remained in the closet. As the minutes passed, he decided he'd been wrong. Maybe the marshal didn't know the old trick of doubling back on your search. He was just about to emerge from the closet when he heard the door burst open.

Francine screamed.

"Oh, excuse me!" Marshal Pike's voice said. "I forgot we'd searched this house already." There was a short silence as he obviously surveyed the room, and then he left. Fargo waited a few minutes more after the sounds of the men's heavy boots had died away in the distance. Then he opened the door of the closet and stepped out.

"That was close," Doc Blair said.

"I owe you," Fargo said. "All of you. You didn't have to believe me."

"We fooled them!" Tommy said gleefully. "But how did you know they were going to come back?"

"That's the first trick of searching," Fargo said. "Just remember that, Tommy. If you have any suspicions, always return and take a surprise second look."

"I ran upstairs to hide the ropes," Francine put in. "I was scrubbing the blood off the floor when they came in to search the room. But I don't think they could tell what it was."

"Quick thinking," Fargo said. He sat down at the table again, and there was an awkward silence. With a shy glance, Francine passed him a thick slice of apple pie.

"What will you do now?" Doc Blair asked, voicing Fargo's thoughts. The marshal had said that in another hour they would have completed searching the town. Then, presumably, they would turn their attention to the countryside around Bentwood, trying to track him.

As these thoughts went through Fargo's head, he picked up the newspaper and scanned the article, hoping to find another clue. The account of Hannah Kempner's death was a lurid one, written as if the writer had witnessed the murder. The killer was called the Mysterious Butcher. Several eyewitnesses claimed that he had come into town the night before and had proceeded to get roaring drunk at the Dusty Rose. Then he insisted on purchasing Hannah for the night and had been shown up to the room. The next morning, so the newspaper said, the madam had discovered him in bed with the poor girl's body stretched out across the floor in her own blood.

Fargo stopped reading at this, his mind reeling. Here was more proof that the story had been written before he had awakened, and that whoever set him up had given the details to the newspaper in advance. Hannah's body had been on the floor when he had awakened, but he had wrapped her in a blanket and put her on the bed before anyone else came into the room.

He read on. The butcher's knife had been discovered beneath the girl's body. Several eyewitnesses identified the knife as the Butcher's because he had flashed it around the saloon the night before.

Now the knife was strapped to Fargo's ankle again. But that wouldn't get him off a death rap. It wasn't proof.

The story went on to say that the madam had summoned the marshal and that the Butcher had escaped by climbing out the window and riding away on his horse.

Fargo sat back and thought. There was nothing about the marshal shooting him, nothing about the murderer being wounded, nothing about crashing through the window, either. And the article was written in a way that such details would surely not have been left out. Fargo knew they were left out because they happened after the newspaper was printed. Once again it didn't help him. But it showed how powerful his unknown enemy was.

The marshal was the most likely suspect. He was a bully, big and powerful. He had seemed to play his part to the hilt, bursting into the room at the Dusty Rose.

"Just who is Marshal Pike?" Fargo asked, stroking his beard.

"I thought you might ask that," Doc Blair said. "He's been in this territory for about a year. Mean son of a bitch. Excuse me, Marilyn. The sheriff can't tolerate him because he's always coming into Bentwood and throwing his weight around, getting in the middle of things, trying to take credit for everything. Pike was pushed in as marshal by Paul Yancey, that show-off would-be governor over in Cheyenne. Yancey seems to be running the politics of the territory now. And it doesn't hurt that Yancey also publishes the *Cheyenne Gazette* and the *Bentwood Times.*"

Fargo felt his hopes rise. Now he was getting somewhere. The marshal was a toady for the real power, this newspaper publisher Paul Yancey in Cheyenne. But the question remained—what was Yancey after?

"And Yancey?" Fargo muttered.

"Don't see much of him," Doc Blair said. "He's rich, powerful. Short man, gray hair and mustache. Real quiet type. But never underestimate Yancey. You wouldn't want to play poker with him."

Fargo sat in deep thought for a moment, and then he rose slowly. His leg and head were still throbbing, but he had become used to the pain. He hardly felt it anymore.

"I guess I'll get on out of town," Fargo said.

"Is . . . is there any way we can help?" Marilyn asked, her wide gray eyes troubled for his safety.

"Yeah, some bullets would help." Fargo drew his Colt and opened it to show them the empty chambers. Marilyn gasped.

"You mean that pistol has been empty all this time?" Francine asked, amazed. Fargo nodded.

"Tommy, fetch that box of bullets from your father's gun closet." Marilyn said. Tommy ran to do her bidding. "And just how do you aim to get out, Skye? This town is as heavily guarded as a prison. The only way you'll get out of here is as a corpse."

Doc hit the table with one hand.

"That gives me an idea!" the doc said. "I know just how I can help you. Not only am I the town doctor, but I'm also the undertaker. I'll just bring around a coffin in a wagon and smuggle you out of town."

"They'll stop and search every wagon on the road," Fargo said. "It won't work."

"Sure it will," Marilyn said, her color rising. "I'll go along. We all will."

"Marilyn," Doc Blair said firmly. "This is going to be dangerous. And besides, you're not well enough to travel."

"Yes I am," she said defiantly, tossing her auburn hair. "And besides, you need a dead body!"

That night Fargo slept in the attic, restlessly. When he awoke and realized that half the morning had gone, he knew how bad off he was. His head felt as heavy as solid lead, and his leg had stiffened. All night his sleep had been disturbed by dreams filled with gunfire and darkness, of running and hiding out. Fargo stretched slowly. He rose and tried to work the stiffness out of his leg. If anything, it felt worse than the day before, even though he knew it was on the mend.

The gravity of his situation struck him. Damn it. Just when he needed all his strength, he was half crippled. And if he could only remember who had set him up . . .

He heard the others moving down below. As he eased himself slowly down the stairs, Fargo realized how lucky he had been to stumble into the Fosters' house. Marilyn and Francine had taken good care of him. And Doc had a plan to smuggle him out of town. The game wasn't over yet, he thought grimly, as his leg hit against the banister and a fresh wave of pain coursed through him. He gritted his teeth and thought of Marshal Pike, which galvanized the pain to anger.

After a couple of hours they were ready to depart. Fargo had loaded the Colt. Doc and Tommy had retrieved Fargo's saddle and bridle hidden in the brush at the edge of town. They had sighted the Ovaro grazing not far away, but it wouldn't come to them. Marilyn and Francine had packed plenty of provisions. The heavy mountain wagon with the canvas top stood waiting at the back door. Inside of it was an empty coffin, the largest and deepest one Doc Blair had on hand.

Doc checked to see that no one was around, and then Marilyn and Fargo slipped out the back door and climbed into the back of the wagon along with Francine. Doc and Tommy climbed onto the front seat.

Fargo settled himself on a pile of blankets, leaning against his saddle and bags. He stretched out his leg before him. A mountain wagon wasn't the fastest way to get to Cheyenne, but it would get them there well before the murdered girl's sister, Lillian Kempner, arrived.

If Marshal Pike and his men came upon them on the trail, Fargo would get into the coffin, covered by Marilyn's cape. Then she would lie down on top of him. The doc was prepared to tell a story about how she took a sudden turn for the worse. And Francine was ready to say that her mother had insisted on being buried in Cheyenne. If Marshal Pike went as far as opening the coffin, they would see Marilyn. It might work, Fargo thought. In any case, it was better than trying to outride the marshal's men with a bad leg. At least for today, he decided.

Doc flapped the reins on the eight-mule team, and the mountain wagon pulled out onto the main street of Bentwood. Fargo inched up the canvas side and looked out at the false-fronted stores as they drove down the street. They passed the Dusty Rose saloon, and a drunken man stumbled out of the bat-wing doors. Wanted Posters were tacked to all the storefronts. He was too far away to read them, but he knew his picture was on every one. They passed a few carriages and men on horseback riding in the opposite direction, but no one seemed to take any notice of them.

In another minute they were out of the town and jouncing along the rutted roadway southward.

Fargo called for the doc to halt, and then he stood in the wagon, leaning out over the driver's seat. He whistled, a low piercing sound that carried for a long way. Then he waited and whistled again. In another moment they heard the pounding of hooves, and the black and white pinto came galloping toward them through the sage.

"That's neat," Tommy said as the horse came up to the wagon. Fargo leaned out and patted the Ovaro's nose.

"The horse will follow us," he said.

"It's just fifteen miles until we meet up with the Oregon Trail," Doc said, starting up the team again. "Then we turn east to Cheyenne."

"There won't be any settlers' wagons on the trail this late in the year," Fargo remarked. "The smart ones will be almost to California by now—or settling in somewhere for the winter. It's just as well, because the fewer people we run into the better."

On either side of the trail, red rocks towered into the blue sky. The rabbit bush was yellow with autumn and lit golden by the afternoon sun. Fargo let down the canvas, lay back, and closed his eyes. But the pain in his head wouldn't let him sleep again.

"Can I do something for you?" Marilyn asked softly. She got up to move nearer to him. For the first time Fargo noticed her willowy body and her high, rounded breasts beneath her flowered cotton dress.

"It's my head," Fargo said. "Still hurting."

Marilyn reached over and began gently massaging

his neck and shoulders. He closed his eyes as her fingers pushed more deeply into his tense muscles. Her hands were firm and yet gentle, probing. She leaned closer to him, and he smelled a whiff of lavender.

"Great," he said softly. He could feel the pain in his head diminishing as his muscles loosened. He drifted down into sleep again.

Marilyn shook him gently awake.

"It's Pike," she whispered.

Fargo came awake immediately. The dusk light filtered into the canvas-covered wagon. Francine had opened the coffin lid, and Fargo quickly lay down in the long pine box. Outside he heard the jangle of horses and hoofbeats as the men drew near. Francine covered him with Marilyn's cape, and then he felt Marilyn's slender soft weight as she hesitantly stretched out on top of him. The coffin was deep enough that the lid could be put back on, even with the two of them lying inside. Francine quickly closed the lid.

Inside the coffin Fargo lay silently, straining to hear what was going on outside. The voices were muffled. Marilyn shifted as she lay on top of him. He felt the curve of her slender hips on his, her soft rear pressing down on him. And he inhaled her scent—lavender and her own essence. Fargo felt himself stirring and knew that Marilyn would feel it, too. He felt her hand drop beside her and lightly stroke his side, once, hesitantly. Then the voices grew louder. Fargo could make out Marshal Pike's gruff rumble.

"Please, don't!" Francine's voice protested as the coffin lid was raised.

"Yeah, she's in there," the marshal said, lowering the lid again quickly. The muffled voices continued for a few minutes and then died away. The mountain wagon lurched forward again, but Fargo and Marilyn didn't move.

"Do you think they'll come to look again?" Marilyn whispered to him.

"I have a feeling they won't this time," Fargo answered her. On the other hand, he could think of worse things than having Marilyn Foster stretched out on top of him in the dark. And he could think of even better things, too. Fargo raised his hands and very slowly caressed her rib cage, hips, and thighs. He felt her shiver. The coffin lid was raised, and Fargo dropped his hands.

"I think they're gone," Francine said.

Marilyn sat up and struggled out of the coffin, followed by Fargo.

"I . . . hope I wasn't too heavy," Marilyn said, unable to meet his eye.

"You were just right," Fargo answered. Francine looked from her mother to Fargo and back again, a slight suspicion on her face.

"Oregon Trail is right ahead," Doc Blair said from the driver's seat. "Time we were camping."

The evening star was ablaze by the time they lit the camp fire and pitched tents in a hollow sheltered with sage and greasewood. Fargo scouted out the area slowly, gradually easing the stiffness from his wounded leg. He could feel an improvement already, he realized. The rest in the wagon had done him good. The doc had been right—riding with the sutured wound would have torn it apart again.

Then he called the Ovaro, which came galloping up to him, nuzzling. Fargo fetched oats from the wagon. The dusk was gathering when the doc approached.

"Beautiful horse," he said appreciatively. "I'd like to talk to you about what the marshal told me when he stopped us." Doc Blair puffed on a pipe and looked across the sage plain. "Apparently there's some Indian trouble east of here—up in the hills."

"Shoshoni? They've been pretty quiet lately."

"That's what I thought, too," the doc said. "Marshal Pike seemed awfully sure we'd be safe if we stayed on the trail."

"Well, we've gotta go through that gap anyway," Fargo said. "Did he say what the trouble was?"

"The Indians are causing the ranchers hell. And it all started up in the last couple of months."

"That's strange," Fargo said. "Usually if they're going to attack, they'll pick off a stray wagon on the trail. I wonder what's got them all riled up?"

Francine called them to supper, and Fargo sat on a log, well away from the fire. If strangers came along, he could easily slip into the sage, unseen. After the meal Doc brought out his pipe. They sat around the dying embers, listening to the coyotes howl. Tommy had fallen asleep, leaning against Francine. Marilyn drew her shawl around her shoulders. Fargo glanced up from the fire to find her looking at him. He smiled at her, and she shyly glanced away.

"I think we'd all better turn in," Doc said at last.

Marilyn rose and wrapped a blanket around Tommy, and Doc carried the boy to the wagon to sleep.

Fargo stood and walked slowly back and forth as the others prepared to bed down in the tents.

"Aren't you . . . planning to sleep?" Marilyn said as she passed him, carrying another blanket from the wagon. Fargo thought he heard a subtle invitation behind the words.

"Not tonight," he said. "Somebody has to stay up and keep watch. I slept most of the afternoon."

Marilyn nodded and made her way to her tent, glancing back as she went.

Fargo spent the first few hours walking slowly up and down beside the red coal camp fire. The stiffness was entirely gone from his leg, but he knew if he rested, it would be back. He wasn't healed by any means, but he could feel that the wound was knitting back together.

By midnight he was tired out. He sat wrapped in a blanket close to the fire, feeding it sticks of greasewood. The coyotes were singing in the distance, and the stars whirled slowly overhead. It was nearly two when he heard a noise from the direction of Marilyn's tent. She emerged in a white billowing nightgown. Fargo rose to meet her and wrapped his blanket about her.

"You all right?" he whispered.

"Yes, fine," she said. "But I can't sleep."

She made her way to the fire and sat down on a log beside it. Fargo sat next to her. She glanced up at him, and he saw the firelight gleam in her wide gray eyes.

Her thick auburn hair, loosened over her shoulders, caught the golden light of the fire.

She was a damned fine woman, Fargo thought to himself—strong and level-headed. She looked so different from the bedridden, gray-faced woman he had first seen.

"It's meant so much for me . . . meeting you," Marilyn said, looking into the fire. "Ever since my husband died, I'd forgotten there were men like you around, brave and strong." She paused and looked at him searchingly.

Fargo leaned over and kissed her, nibbling on her lips. She moaned softly as he slid his arms around her. She tasted of oranges, sunny and sweet. He darted his tongue into her mouth, exploring. His hands rubbed her narrow arched back.

"Yes, yes," she gasped. She buried her face in his chest. "Oh, Skye. Until yesterday I just wanted to die. I lay in that bed, miserable and unhappy, month after month, wishing we had never come to Bentwood. Everything seemed so hopeless. But then, when you decided to help that poor girl Lillian and . . . suddenly I realized there were important things to do in the world. I realize I've been missing out on life. Suddenly I feel alive again. And, I'm . . . I'm hungry, Skye."

He leaned over and kissed her again, deeply, holding nothing back as she came up to meet him passionately, her mouth welcoming. Fargo cupped his hands over her high full breasts and felt her shudder under his touch, panting.

"Yes, yes. It's been so long."

Fargo rose and led her from the fire a short distance away into the sagebrush until he reached a small clearing. There he spread the blanket on the ground. He kissed her again, deeply and felt her coming alive, warm and vibrant beneath his hands, responding to his every touch. She unbuttoned his shirt, sliding her warm hands across his broad, muscular chest. Then she lay down on the blanket, and despite the cold night air, she pulled off her nightdress, revealing first her long, shapely legs, the dark triangle of fur between her legs, her slim hips and narrow waist, and finally her mounded white breasts, the nipples erect in the cold night air.

Fargo gazed down at her stretched out on the blanket, her pale lithe body lit by the starlight. He dropped his gunbelt beside the blanket, undid his Levi's, and stripped them off. Marilyn caught her breath.

Fargo lay down beside her, tickling her up one side with his fingertips, circling her breasts and her pubis, teasing. She began to shudder and then clutched at him, her hands strong against his back, pulling him on top of her. Fargo kissed her again, plunging his tongue deeply into her as she guided him inside her snug warmth.

"Oh! Oh!" she gasped as he stroked deeply into her, feeling her come alive around him, bucking up under him and meeting him, stroke her stroke. He bent down and took one nipple between his lips, teasing and pulling.

Marilyn stifled a cry. Fargo reached beneath her and cupped her buttocks, pulling her toward him with each lunge deeper within her. She was warm, comforting, and welcoming. Then he reached one hand between them and gently touched her folded wetness. She moaned with the unbearable pleasure, and he felt her tighten as he swelled larger, the explosion mounting at his base. She thrust harder against him as he touched her seemingly everywhere, inside and out, as if he had taken all of her inside him, and she had taken him in as well. With a shudder he felt her release, and he let himself shoot up inside her, pumping again and again, spending all of himself into his woman beneath him under the stars on the cold earth.

He slowly lowered himself onto her, drawing the blanket around them as he became aware of the creeping cold night air. He kissed her eyelids, her parted lips, the tip of her nose.

"Oh, Skye, thank you. You've brought me back to life."

"You seemed pretty alive to me, Marilyn," he said.

Suddenly he heard, or rather felt through the ground, an approaching horse. He motioned Marilyn to be quiet and quickly got to his feet where he stood, straining his ears toward the sound. It was still distant, but it was coming on. Fargo struggled into his clothes and grabbed his Colt as Marilyn got into her nightdress and wrapped the blanket about her.

Fargo crept back toward the camp fire, with Marilyn following, just as the stranger came into view and began to call out to them.

"Hallo! Hallo! Don't shoot!"

The stranger's horse stumbled down into the hollow. The man had his hands raised in the air. Fargo stepped back from the camp fire, his face obscured in shadow.

"I don't mean trouble," the man said quickly as Fargo raised his Colt to cover him. "I just saw your fire."

"Get down," Fargo said. The man did as he was told and touched the brim of his hat toward Marilyn, who stood by the fire, wrapped in the blanket. Fargo listened to the night. He didn't hear anyone else approaching. Not yet, anyway. Sometimes strangers came into camp and, as soon as your guard was down, the rest of the gang would rush in. That was the usual trick. Fargo heard the doc stirring from his tent.

"What's going on?" Doc Blair said. He came running toward the fire, pistol in hand.

"Who are you?" Fargo asked.

"Name's Mort Godfrey."

Fargo took a long look at the man, a rancher from the dust-stained clothes and sun-whitened Levi's. Godfrey had curly brown hair, an open honest face, and deep laugh lines etched around his mouth.

"What the hell are you doing riding into this camp in the middle of the night?"

"Sorry, but I been riding hell-bent from my ranch. We got Shoshoni trouble out there."

"We heard about that from Marshal Pike," Fargo said. "But why the night ride?"

"I'm heading to Bentwood to round up some more help. Something bad happened," Mort Godfrey said. "Last night the Shoshoni attacked us in the middle of the night—worse then ever before. And they killed the sheriff of Bentwood."

"Sheriff O'Toole?" Doc Blair exclaimed in dismay.

"That's the one," Mort answered. "He'd been helping us fight 'em for the last couple of weeks. He seemed to think there was something funny going on. I think there's always something funny going on with Indians."

"He was a fine man, fine man," Doc Blair said sorrowfully. "Best sheriff we ever had around these parts."

But Fargo hardly heard him as his thoughts whirled. "You say you were attacked at night?" Fargo asked. "Indians aren't night fighters."

"That's what we thought, too," Mort said. "But they've been wiping out the ranchers one by one. The attacks come in waves every couple of days. This was just particularly nasty."

"Are we in danger?" Marilyn asked, shivering.

"I doubt it," Fargo assured her.

"Pike said the Indians weren't attacking travelers—only ranchers," Fargo said. "Still, we'll be on guard."

"Tie up your horse and have some coffee," Doc Blair said. Fargo wished silently that he hadn't. The longer Mort Godfrey hung around, the more likely he'd catch a glimpse of Fargo's face. And if he'd seen one of the wanted posters . . .

Mort made himself comfortable on a rock and took a cup of steaming coffee gratefully. Doc and Marilyn sat near the fire while Fargo remained standing in the shadows, listening to their conversation but with one ear cocked to the sounds of the night beyond the circle of firelight. Except for the coyotes, the night remained quiet.

" . . . so I guess I ought to just sell off my land and get the hell out once and for all," Mort Godfrey was saying. "If the Indians don't leave us alone, we can't get the ranching done. Ain't worth it. I heard of somebody in Cheyenne, willing to buy useless ranch land. Guess I'll sell out to him. It's a damn shame. I've liked it in Windy Gap."

Fargo felt a flash of something like lightning in his head at the words . . . *Windy Gap.* He almost shouted as he remembered. Windy Gap. He'd been there. Something bad was going on. Something he had tried to stop and then . . . He remembered a circle of men around a camp fire . . . the faces. He shook his head as the memory faded.

Well, it was coming back, Fargo thought. His memory was returning bit by bit. But, damn, would it return soon enough?

4

Windy Gap, Windy Gap. The words echoed through Fargo's mind for the rest of the long night. After Mort Godfrey rode on to Bentwood to summon help, Doc and Marilyn had returned to their tents. In the darkness Fargo paced again beside the fire, the dull pain still shooting down his wounded leg, as he tried to reconstruct his memories of Windy Gap. All the while his keen hearing monitored the sounds of the night, the burrowing owls, the coyotes, and the rustle of the night wind.

Windy Gap—Fargo remembered bleak hills and flat buff meadowland between, a shadowy pass and the Rockies rising tall on the near horizon. Ranchers, their faces ravaged with worries, around a camp fire. That image floated before him again. He'd been to Windy Gap recently, talking to the ranchers. And he remembered another face, a long narrow face with large eyes whose lower lids hung loose like an old dog's. The man had had thin, brown spiderlike hands and a tall lanky frame. The dog-faced man had called him over to talk about . . .

Here the memory faded. Fargo clutched at it, then

gave up. But he felt certain that whatever had happened in Windy Gap was connected with the girl's murder at the Dusty Rose. And Dogface was part of it. But how? Well, at least he was beginning to remember.

At first light Fargo threw more greasewood on the fire and made a pot of coffee. The warm odor awoke Doc Blair, who came stumbling out of his tent, scratching at his graying head. He went immediately to the camp fire and poured himself a cup.

"I've got to head out to Windy Gap." Fargo said without preamble.

Doc looked up at him, startled.

"What for?"

"I don't know," Fargo said, stroking his bearded chin. "But I know it's connected to Hannah's murder. I can't remember just how."

"So, you're starting to get your memory back," Doc Blair said. "But you're in no condition—"

"I'll be fine," Fargo said. "The leg's much better now."

Just then they heard one of the others stirring. In a moment Marilyn appeared. Today she had caught back her thick auburn hair in a bow, and a blue blouse and buckskin skirt clung to her slenderness.

She smiled broadly as she made her way to the fire, then she gave Fargo a kiss on the cheek and bent down to get a cup of coffee. Doc Blair threw Fargo a surprised and bemused glance.

"You're looking better today, Marilyn," Doc Blair said, a twinkle in his eye. "Why, if I didn't know better, I'd swear you were in the pink of health."

Marilyn laughed delightedly. "It's this fresh air and getting out of bed," she said merrily, tossing her auburn hair. "And the company." She flashed a smile at Fargo. "So, when do we get going for Cheyenne?"

Doc Blair exchanged looks with Fargo and then excused himself, making for the tents. Marilyn watched him leave.

"I'm not going on to Cheyenne," Fargo said. Marilyn's face blanched. She started to protest, and he laid a finger on her lips.

"When that rancher came in last night and mentioned Windy Gap, I knew it was connected to the murder. I'm going to ride out there today and see what's up. Then I'll head back to Cheyenne—alone. I'll still make it in time to meet Lillian's stagecoach."

Marilyn glanced away from him, looking out over the rolling white sage. Tears started in her eyes. "I knew it wouldn't be forever, but I . . . didn't know it would be so short."

"Neither did I," Fargo said gently, taking her into his arms. He kissed her deeply, tasting the now familiar sweet orange flavor of her mouth, smelling the lavender scent in her hair.

"We could come to Windy Gap with you!" she suddenly said.

"I couldn't let you do that," Fargo said. "The Shoshoni are all over the place. A lot of men have been killed. It's no place for you."

She nodded as one tear rolled down her cheek. "Just promise you'll come back through Bentwood."

"Sometime I will," Fargo said. "I promise. But just promise me you'll lay low in Bentwood for a while.

Marshal Pike is going to be mighty suspicious if he sees you've been raised from the dead. It might be a week, maybe two, until I get this straightened out. I'll send word when it's safe."

"I understand," Marilyn said. "I'll stay out of sight till then—with a lot of nice memories." She stood on tiptoe to kiss him once and then hurried away toward the tent.

Fargo watched as she disappeared. Then he whistled for the Ovaro, which galloped up in a moment. Fargo was just saddling it when Doc ambled toward the fire.

"You really meaning to go into Windy Gap?"

Fargo nodded. Doc changed the bandage on the leg one last time and then gave him extra bandages and a glass vial of morphine in case the pain started up again. Fargo mounted easily and looked down at the doc.

"I appreciate everything you've done—getting the bullet out of my leg and getting me out of Bentwood."

"Didn't have a choice about the first," Doc said with a rueful grin. "And as to the second, I don't know we did you any favors, what with Marshal Pike and his men still scouring the countryside for you."

Fargo nodded. "I'll be careful. I plan to ride well off the trail. They won't find me. Tell Francine and Tommy good-bye for me."

Doc Blair waved as Fargo galloped off.

The white sage was a blur beneath him as he headed down the trail. The black and white pinto's taut muscles propelled them over the rugged ground. A mile south of the main trail, Fargo came across an older track, parallel tracks cut deep by wagons some years before. He turned onto the track and galloped west, the miles flying beneath them hour after hour. The horse seemed happy to have him in the saddle again, and it ran on and on, seemingly tireless.

The land changed gradually as they climbed, the flats of white sage and greasewood giving way to rough hills dappled with scrub oak and junipers. The land lay wide around, the horizon undulating with the line of the Rockies to the west and the south. The Oregon Trail followed the line of the North Platte River and then headed through a gap in the high hills on the way to South Pass. It was the easiest passage through the Rockies north of Santa Fe. After South Pass the trail split, and the Oregon Trail continued northwest, while the Mormon Trail went to the great lake of salt and the California Trail led to Sutter's Fort.

Near sunset, at the top of a tall ridge, Fargo reined in and looked around. Low gray clouds scudded across the blue sky, and the sun shone intermittently. A brisk autumn wind lifted the Ovaro's long mane. Spread out below him, Fargo could see the high hills around Windy Gap and the trail cutting across the grass-bound land next to the rocky-banked North Platte River. The bleak hills and bluffs rising around were impassable. Any wagon traveling west had to pass through Windy Gap, or else make a hundred-mile detour to the north. And the land of the Gap, rich flat bottomland, was perfect for cattle.

As Fargo looked down at the scene, he felt memory prick at him again. He remembered riding these hills, looking for something. It must have been the

Shoshoni, he told himself. He let the Ovaro walk forward slowly down the slope toward Windy Gap. The sinking sun splashed red across the sky.

Fargo realized he was bone-weary. The leg was starting to throb again. And, after a sleepless night keeping watch and a full day in the saddle, he needed rest. It was nearly dark when he stopped on the rocky banks of the North Platte River. Fargo dismounted and let the pinto drink long. He filled his hat and dashed the chilled water over his face.

He would have to find a safe protected spot for the night now. Rest was necessary, or he would make mistakes. Just then he stiffened, his sixth sense telling him danger was near. The pinto had wandered into the river and was drinking. It raised its head with a snort. Man and horse smelled danger approaching.

Fargo drew his Colt and listened, turning his head from one side to the other. The high red bluff echoed the faint sound of jangling spurs and horse's hooves. The sound seemed to come from all directions. Fargo swore.

The pinto came out of the water, dripping, and Fargo swung onto its back and listened again. The sound still seemed to come from both sides of him. Danger, it seemed, lay in either direction.

Fargo took a chance and headed upstream, deeper into Windy Gap. The brush was thick, but low on either side of the river as the gap narrowed. The running water reflected the last of the daylight in the sky above. At a turning, beneath a mammoth overhanging bluff, Fargo paused and listened again. The sound of spurs and horses came once more, men's voices, too, and close. Behind him the sounds increased. So, it wasn't just the reflected sound off the rocks. There were two parties of men approaching, heading straight for him. And he was now in a narrow part of the canyon, with high cliff walls and no cover. His best chance was to get across the river into the thick brush on the other side, which would be just tall enough to hide him and the horse.

The Ovaro plunged into the river and forded quickly. They were halfway across when Fargo realized he had made a fatal error. The men were closer than he had thought, impossible to hear because of the high rocks reflecting the sound. Suddenly a shout rang out, and Fargo turned in his saddle to see a dozen riders coming around the bluff. They reined in when they spotted him and peered at him through the gathering gloom. The second party arrived an instant later from the opposite direction, galloping around a stand of low brush. Marshal Pike was in the lead.

Pike pulled up in astonishment. Fargo realized in a flash that even if the gathering darkness hid his face at this distance, the distinctive black and white markings of the pinto were unmistakable.

"The Butcher!" the marshal shouted. "Get him, boys!"

Both groups were just out of rifle range, but they drew and advanced as they began to fire. Fargo urged the pinto onward. A moment later a bullet kicked up a fan of water and another barely missed his ear as he hunched low on the horse. He looked ahead and realized the situation was hopeless. Even if he made it to the brush on the opposite riverbank, it wouldn't hide him from the battering gunfire. And the horse was a large target. It would be only a matter of moments before one of the bullets hit the faithful pinto. Just as he came up to the riverbank, another bullet zinged close by, and Fargo sat bolt upright, then flung himself from the saddle. He hit the water with a huge splash and was thankful it was just deep enough that he didn't scrape the skin off his face. He felt one hoof of the Ovaro brush past him as he pulled his body down flat into the freezing water and, holding his breath, crawled toward the center of the river, where it was deepest, and let the current carry him swiftly downriver.

Around him he could hear dimly the slight swoosh as bullets tore into the water around him. Gradually the shots grew fewer and fewer. Fargo opened his eyes under water, but there was too little light to see anything. The men would figure they shot him, and if he was still alive, he'd have crawled back onto the riverbank. Fargo's lungs were burning and spots of light danced before his eyes whether he had them open or not. The current pulled him downstream, dashing him against the submerged rocks again and again until he was battered, while he struggled to keep his body submerged.

Blackness began to well up, and he knew he would have to get air. He wedged himself against a large rock to steady himself against the current and let his head come up slowly, so that just his face came up out of the river. He drew in a long silent breath, which made his head swim worse than before. In another couple of breaths it began to clear. Fargo cautiously raised his head another inch and blinked the water out of his eyes. Just ten feet away one of the marshal's men was riding in the shallows, gazing searchingly at the riverbank, his back to Fargo.

Just then Fargo felt a scratch and nudge from behind. He turned instinctively and lashed out—a tangle of branches and matted leaves had floated up behind him. His motion made a splash and he felt, rather than saw, the searcher turn toward the sound. Fargo swore inwardly and ducked his head again into the cold water. With one hand he let go of the rock while he held the tangle of weeds with the other, moving with it downstream. After a half minute he came up again, pushing aside the matted leaves and poking his head up inside the tangled branches.

He looked about slowly. On either side of the dark riverbanks the mounted men were riding back and forth, searching the brush, sometimes firing into it. Fargo floated down the center of the stream, keeping his body beneath the surface of the water.

"I think we must have killed him," one of the men shouted. "He sure ain't anywhere on the banks."

"Keep looking!" Pike's voice rang out. "That bastard's here somewhere."

Fargo continued to float downstream until the men's voices were distant and far behind him. After a half mile he decided to venture out. He made his way toward the tangled brush on the bank slowly and, after a long, hard look around, hauled himself out of the freezing water.

The night air blew cold on his wet clothes. Fargo swore. Great. Here he was in the middle of the night with no horse, no supplies, and soaking wet. And his leg was stiffening up bad.

He stood and looked about slowly. He could still hear an occasional shout from upstream. The best thing would be to get far away from the river as quickly as possible.

Fargo crossed the grassy flat beside the river and climbed the gentle hogback. From the top he looked down again. The moon was rising full in the east, and the silver light poured over the still valley. He could no longer hear or see the men behind him. But he did see something else—a flash of white on the grassy plain below. Or did he? Fargo cupped his hands and whistled, low. The night air seemed to blow the eerie sound back at him. He tried again, straining his eyes to follow the flash of white. In another moment he knew it was the pinto who had heard his call.

In a few minutes the Ovaro was galloping up the hillside toward him. Fargo leaped on its back and plunged down the other side of the hogback. They would find a spot to make camp far from the river. With the swim and the long ride, he was exhausted and could feel it creeping along his limbs.

He headed toward a low saddle covered with juniper and scrub oak, hoping there would be a refuge on the far side. When he gained the top and looked down, he saw that he was wrong.

Below him was a protected valley, washed by moonlight. A few low, dark buildings stood here and there. And a large camp fire was lit outside, with men moving around it.

Fargo was about to turn away, when he remembered. This was where he had been—in this valley, with these men at Windy Gap, around that camp fire. Something had happened there that set off the murder at the Dusty Rose. Somehow, it was connected. But that was all he could recall. His clothes had nearly dried on him, blown by the cold night air. All he really wanted was a fire and some hot coffee and a warm bedroom. But he realized that night was his best friend. In the daylight it would be harder for him to find out what was going on. He had to keep going.

Fargo reined the pinto toward a long line of juniper that skittered down raggedly toward the valley floor. By the time he'd reached the last tree, he could hear the men's voices around the camp fire, even though he couldn't make out the words.

He dismounted, leaving the horse near the last tree. Then, crouching, he ran forward, pausing here and there in the cover of brush. He had to circle around a couple of men standing and smoking—not very effective sentries. And, eventually, he made his way closer to the golden fire.

Finally he crouched in a stand of chokecherry where he could clearly hear what the men were saying.

" . . . well, I still say Marshal Pike knows what he's doing," a deep bass voice rumbled.

"And I say he can't do nothing about these savages," another voice put in. "It'll be just like last time. The Shoshoni will attack somebody's ranch, and Pike and his men will be miles away."

"That's why I say we gotta do it ourselves," another voice said.

Fargo crept forward on his belly, keeping hidden among the grasses. He was close enough to make out the faces of the men around the fire. He recognized the ranchers of Windy Gap. That much he remembered. But Dogface was not among them.

Just then he heard the hooves of several horses coming down the slope. The watchers gave the alarm, and the men at the camp fire all came to their feet, rifles at the ready. Fargo shrank lower into the grass as the riders passed nearby.

"Having a little party here?" Marshal Pike's voice boomed out.

"Just trading some news," one of the ranchers answered shortly. It was clear from his tone, he didn't hold Pike in much esteem.

"I ran into the marshal on the trail," one of the men said as he dismounted. Fargo recognized Mort Godfrey, the man who had stumbled into their camp the night before. "I didn't even have to ride to Bentwood."

"Yep," Pike said boastfully. "We heard you were having some more trouble up here, so we came to help out. And on the way here, we bagged that butcher."

Even from a distance Fargo could see the ranchers shift uncomfortably. Marshal Pike didn't seem to take any notice.

"Shot the bastard full of holes," another man, obviously from Pike's group, said boastfully. "Fell in the river. He's probably floated halfway Missouri by now."

There was a long silence.

"Anyway, we'll get them savages," Pike said vehemently. "That is, if they attack again. Would be a pity if I get my boys all the way up in these hills and those redskins don't show."

No one answered. Pike remounted.

"You ranchers is just lucky you've got somebody like Paul Yancey to watch out for you." Fargo started at the name, remembering the doc's description of the rich powerful publisher in Cheyenne. "Yancey can't make the redskins stop attacking you immediately. But believe me, he's going to do everything he can to help."

The men muttered among themselves as Marshal Pike wheeled about and galloped with the several others back up the slope. The ranchers talked on for a while longer and then began to drift away, mounting and riding off into the night.

Fargo watched the group carefully, keeping an eye on Mort Godfrey's figure. When the rancher got up to leave, Fargo noted that he rode a bright white horse. Fargo backed away silently and quickly retraced his steps to the Ovaro, skirting the sentinels who were now walking toward the camp fire. Fargo mounted and followed Mort's horse in the distance, heading across the wide valley. Other mounted men were heading toward the hogback, several passing quite near. None of the ranchers took any notice of him as he rode after Mort, assuming he was one of them.

After about three miles Mort Godfrey galloped through a narrow passage between two bluffs. Fargo paused and looked upward at the towering rocks. If this was the passage to Mort's ranch, it was certainly well chosen and eminently defensible. With a prickle of caution he moved the Ovaro through very slowly. Just at the end of the passageway, a grass-bottomed canyon opened up before him.

"Freeze," Mort's voice rang out from the deep darkness of a nearby juniper. "I got you covered."

"Friend," Fargo said, raising his hands slowly. "We met on the Oregon Trail."

"You again?" Mort's voice said questioningly. "Alone?"

"Yep," Fargo answered.

"Why were you following me?" Mort asked.

"I've got some questions about what the hell is going on around here," Fargo said. Fargo felt the man relax slightly, but he didn't lower the rifle. The barrel gleamed blue in the moonlight, but Mort was hidden in shadow.

"What's your name, anyway?" Mort asked.

"Skye Fargo."

There was a long silence.

Fargo instinctively felt the pull of the trigger an instant before Mort's rifle spit fire and the bullet whizzed past him as he dove sideways, rolling over. He gathered his feet under him and sprang with a cry toward Godfrey. The rifle exploded again, the shot flying wide as Fargo hit the man, knocking him off his feet. They rolled over and over down a short rise as Mort's fists pounded him. Fargo sank his left into Mort's gut, and his breath left him in a whoosh, the punches suddenly ceasing. They came to a halt, and Fargo pinioned Mort's arms to the ground. His face was inches from the rancher's. The moonlight brushed Mort's features, and Fargo saw hatred there.

"Why the hell did you kill that girl?" Mort raged. "You bastard!" Godfrey struggled under Fargo's iron grip to no avail.

"I didn't," Fargo said. "It was a setup. Somebody knocked me out and put me in there with the dead girl. When I woke up, there she was."

Mort stopped struggling as Fargo's words sank in.

"Well, if you didn't kill her, then who did?"

"That's what I'm trying to find out," Fargo said. "But you seem to know my name. Have we met before I ran into you on the trail?"

"Don't play games with me, Fargo!" Godfrey spat.

"I'm not," Fargo said. "This may be hard to believe, but whoever knocked me out did such a fine job that I can't remember what happened for the several days before. That Doc Blair, who was with me back on the trail? He told me it was amnesia . . . forgetfulness."

Godfrey whistled low.

"Well, that explains a lot. If you're telling the truth."

"Of course it's the truth. Because otherwise it's a helluva hare-brained lie!"

Godfrey relaxed and laughed.

"Well, that it is, Fargo. I'm half inclined to believe you, because otherwise you wouldn't dare show yourself around here. In any case you can let me up. I'm not going to shoot at you again."

Fargo got to his feet slowly, keeping an eye on

Mort. Godfrey dusted himself off, then looked up at the moonlit figure of Skye Fargo.

"Yep, it's you all right. You got some explaining to do. I should have recognized you back on the trail, except you kept yourself in the shadows. And I was in too much of a hurry to give it much thought. But we heard tonight that you'd gotten killed over in the river."

"Yeah, I heard Marshal Pike tell you that," Fargo said. Mort stared in astonishment. "I was twenty yards away in the middle of a bush. Well, Pike thought he got me. But then, he thought he had me back in Bentwood when he busted into the room and found me with that poor murdered girl."

Even in the moonlight Fargo saw Mort stiffen at the mention of the girl.

"Do you think . . . Pike is mixed up in that?" Mort asked.

"There's no question in my mind," Fargo answered. "But I've got a lot of questions for you. A lot of things I can't remember."

"Let's get on inside," Mort said. "My ranch ain't fancy, but we'll get a good fire going and a nice pot of coffee."

Fargo brought the Ovaro forward and walked with Mort toward the small ranch house in the middle of the grassy meadow. In the still night Fargo could hear the mournful lowing of cattle some distance away.

"Sounds like a good-size herd."

"Yep."

Mort opened the gate of the corral and unsaddled his big white, patting it affectionately as it trotted into the enclosure. Fargo removed the bridle and saddle from the Ovaro, then slapped its withers and it ran free.

"You don't pen up that horse?" Mort asked curiously as he closed the gate and turned to watch the black and white pinto canter easily across the meadow.

"Marshal Pike knows my horse. If he checks by tonight, we sure don't want that pinto standing in your corral."

Mort nodded and led the way to the ranch house.

The wood stove was stoked and red-hot, the coffee and beans steaming. Fargo bathed in a bucket of warm water and changed into fresh, thoroughly dry clothes from his saddlebags. Before putting on clean Levi's, Fargo sat on a wooden chair and slowly unwound the still moist bandages from his thigh. He hoped he wouldn't see any seepage or infection. He'd spent the day in hard riding, and the wound might have torn open again. He was glad to see that the doc's stitches had held well. And although the wound was tender and red, there was no unusual swelling. It was healing cleanly.

Mort Godfrey, putting tin plates on the rough table, caught sight of Fargo's leg and whistled.

"Bear get you?"

"Yeah," Fargo said slowly. "One named Pike."

Fargo rebandaged the wound and finished dressing, then sat down at the table with the rancher. They dug into the dish of beef and beans. When they had finished and were drinking coffee, Godfrey spoke again.

"We got our own problems with Marshal Pike."

"How's that?" Fargo asked.

"Some of us ranchers feel he ain't really doing anything to help against the Shoshoni. He brings his men in here and makes a big show of how he's going to protect us, but the ranches keep being attacked."

"Are the Indians picking off your cattle?"

"Nah," Mort said. "The Shoshoni come in the middle of the night and murder anybody they can. Sometimes they take scalps. The ones that don't get killed don't want to stick around. So there's a lot of deserted ranches around. Hell, I'm thinking of selling out. Going somewhere there's less trouble."

Fargo nodded thoughtfully.

"The whole thing's confusing. That's why we asked you to help us."

"What?" Fargo started.

"Yep. Guess you don't remember that, either. You came riding through. Ran into Jake Slade just down the mountain. Told him who you were and he brought you to meet with us—"

"Around a camp fire one night," Fargo interrupted, the memory coming back now. "We talked about getting organized to battle the Shoshoni, maybe approaching the chief for a treaty. Everybody seemed real willing."

"Sure, we were willing. You told us you'd do the job for us for a fee. We forked it over, too. Then we never saw you again."

"Hell," Fargo said. The memory was coming back slowly. "How much did you pay me?"

"A thousand. Split among ten ranchers."

"Now I remember the money, but it's pretty foggy."

Fargo sat for a long moment, looking down at the table. "Goddamn it," he added, almost to himself.

"After you disappeared with our money, next thing we heard was that you murdered . . . I didn't want to believe it at first. I mean, you got a helluva good reputation. But, then we saw the wanted posters and somebody brought a newspaper from Bentwood. And I figured they must be right. But, actually, I'd rather listen to my gut. And my gut tells me you're telling the truth. I just hope whoever killed Hannah is caught." Mort pounded the table with one fist.

"You knew her?" Fargo asked.

"My partner and I were both sweet on her once upon a time. He was just a kid, name of Harry Joe Kline. Well, she picked him over me, no hard feelings. But six months ago these Indian attacks started, and Harry was one of the first to get killed. Hannah was hysterical, and she thought he'd been murdered by somebody, not the Indians. She must have been out of her mind with grieving because the next thing I knew she'd taken up the sporting life at the Dusty Rose. Never could figure her out."

Fargo sat and thought for a long moment.

"Maybe she had no choice about working at the Dusty Rose."

"Hell, Hannah?" Mort snorted. "Any dozen men would've married her right off the bat, me among them."

"Or maybe she worked there to find out something about . . . what did you say his name was again?"

"Harry Joe Kline, God rest his soul."

Fargo reached into his pocket and brought the small

opal ring out with the initials inscribed inside. Mort's eyes widened as it saw it.

"I thought maybe the initials inside made the ring from Hannah's sister, Lillian. But more likely it was from Harry."

Mort nodded sorrowfully.

"Before she died," Fargo continued, "Hannah wrote a letter to her sister, Lillian. She said she had 'proof' of something and that she was being watched. Maybe it has to do with what's going on here at Windy Gap. Maybe not. Anyway, I plan to get to Cheyenne to meet Lillian's stagecoach. And I hope whoever murdered Hannah doesn't beat me to it."

"I'd like to go with you, Fargo," Mort said simply. "I loved Hannah, and I hate to see her sister in danger. I'd like to help you get to the bottom of this."

"There is one thing I do remember clearly," Fargo said after a time. "There was a man sitting by the camp fire with a long, narrow face, like an old dog's. I didn't see him there tonight."

"I remember the one you mean. Name of . . . Joe Johnson, I think, Yeah, he was some new rancher, just moved in. Came to a couple of our meetings. Now that I think about it, after you disappeared, we didn't see him again neither."

Fargo sat back and propped his boots near the wood stove, the thoughts spinning in his mind. His memory was returning, and the pieces were starting to fit together, but he still couldn't see what the puzzle meant. Drowsiness began to cover him like a dark blanket. At last they got up from the fire and made their way to the two camp beds in the bunk room. Fargo took off his boots, undid his holster, lay back on the blanket, and was instantly asleep.

A soft thump awoke him.

Fargo lay for a long moment in the strange cot, trying to remember where he was. Then he heard it again. He was on his feet in an instant, buckling the holster about him silently. He pulled on his boots as he heard the noise again—a soft thump coming from outside the thick log walls of the ranch house.

Fargo stole across to the cot where Mort lay sleeping and touched him on the shoulder. The rancher was awake instantly.

"Trouble. Outside."

Mort rose, slid into his boots, and grabbed his rifle. Fargo slipped to the one small window in the room and peered out into the night. The moonlight washed across the meadow and the tall bluffs. All was still. Then Fargo spotted the men coming. He peered into the darkness. They were wearing headdresses. Shoshoni.

And they were coming on in a long line.

In an instant Fargo wondered what the thump had been, but then his view was blocked as a huge man in buckskins suddenly stood up from where he'd been crouching beneath the window. The dark figure raised a tomahawk above his head to smash in the window.

5

Fargo drew and blasted his Colt, which spit fire into the darkness. The window shattered, and the huge warrior, his tomahawk raised, jolted backward with the impact of the bullet as it hit dead center in his chest. Fargo heard confused shouts from men beyond and then shooting erupted.

"Cover the other window!" Fargo shouted at Mort. The ranch house had one window in each of its two rooms. The bullets struck against the side of the log house. One whizzed by Fargo's head as he ducked and came up again, firing his Colt through the broken window at the points of fire coming from the Shoshoni guns.

Fargo ducked to reload. Indians usually attacked at dawn or during daylight. And these were firing from fixed positions, not riding in close on their mounts. The whole thing was strange. Fargo grabbed his Sharps rifle and popped off a few more shots, hearing one Indian scream in agony as a bullet found its mark. In the moonlight it was hard to discern the Indians crawling forward in the long grasses. But their guns gave them away every time they fired. Mort Godfrey was firing off round after round.

"How are you doing in there?" Fargo shouted during a momentary pause in the gun battle.

"Got grazed on my shoulder, but I'm still spitting bullets!" Mort shouted back.

The silence lingered for a few moments. Fargo peered out into the moonlight landscape. The figures of the Indians were indistinct in the darkness.

"What do you suppose they're up to?" he asked Mort.

"Maybe sneaking up on the sides where I didn't put any windows."

In another moment it became all too clear what they were up to. First Fargo's keen sense of smell caught a vague whiff of smoke. The smell intensified and then quickly became overpowering. A dim flicker of firelight crossed the yard like moving shadows. Fargo heard the ominous crackle of flames consuming dry wood.

"The bastards set fire to my roof!" Mort swore. "They're going to burn us out!"

Fargo looked hastily about. Two windows and one door—no escape—and a whole tribe of bloodthirsty Shoshoni waiting outside with rifles ready to pick them off when it got too hot. Now what the hell could they do? The gunfire began again, fitfully. Fargo sighted several men. Two had come up on their elbows out of the grass, less cautious now as they watched their quarry burn. Fargo fired two shots from his Sharps in quick succession, and the two men flinched and then lay still.

Meanwhile the fire on the roof was roaring, sputtering, and crackling. It was getting hot inside the ranch house, and the smoke was thick. Fargo's eyes watered from the acrid smoke. He pulled his kerchief over his nose. They couldn't hold out much longer inside the cabin.

Fargo scanned the room again, then noticed Mort's kitchen table. It was an unusual piece of furniture, a six-inch slab of wood on stocky legs. Immediately Fargo knew they had a chance—a slim one, though.

Calling to Mort, Fargo left the window and quickly stood the heavy table on end. The thick wood might stop the bullets at that range or might not. But it was a helluva lot better than being roasted alive.

The heat was now blasting hot. At Fargo's instructions, Mort flung open the front door. A gust of fresh air and a hail of bullets poured in. The Indians shouted to one another, sure of victory. A loud crack resounded through the ranch house, and Fargo felt it shudder. He turned back to see the roof of the bunk room beginning to cave in. The heat blasted them. There was no time to lose.

Fargo pushed the table forward, standing it on one end as a shield. Mort took position beside him as they maneuvered it awkwardly toward the gaping door. Fargo felt the bullets' impact, but none penetrated the half foot of solid wood.

They continued to push the table in front of them, balanced vertically until they were clear of the door and a few feet in front of the burning ranch house. At Fargo's signal they suddenly let it fall sideways to form a front barrier three feet tall, behind which they huddled together.

Fargo realized they were vulnerable along both sides, with no protection. They blasted away at the Indians to each side of them, keeping up the offensive. The night wind blew burning shingles down from the roof, and Fargo felt the heat blast his back, until he wondered if his clothes would catch fire and his skin blister. They popped up one after another, winging more of the Indians.

"We can't hold this position for long," Fargo said as he plugged one Shoshoni off to the side.

"Got any more ideas?" Mort asked.

"I think we'll have to make a run for it," Fargo said. "You cover me while I go for the shed and take cover behind those barrels. Then you come on over. That will put us nearer the corral."

"Yeah," Mort said. "With a lot of luck . . . "

Fargo dashed forward, leaping from side to side as he ran, crouched low, the bullets thudding into the earth around him and burning through the air. He crashed into the side wall of the shed and threw himself behind the barrels standing there. After a moment he pulled his rifle up.

The ranch house was a blaze of red and gold fire rising high and roaring into the night sky. The rising black smoke obscured the stars above. Fargo poured a fusillade of bullets toward the encircling Indians, firing his Colt, then his Sharps. Mort leaped over the table and dashed toward him. He almost made it, but a bullet whizzed by, catching him in the shoulder. Mort hit the dirt.

Fargo leaned out amidst the zinging shots and pulled Mort to cover. Then, with the barrel of his Sharps, he retrieved Mort's rifle, which had fallen from his grasp.

"Hell!" Mort shouted, holding his shoulder in agony. "It . . . ain't in . . . my chest," he added through gritted teeth.

"All right, now we gotta get to the corral," Fargo said.

But the Shoshoni had already figured out that's what they intended. Fargo heard the direction of their fire change. Then he heard a sound he hated almost above any other—the scream of a wounded horse, a mortally wounded horse. Fargo rose up from behind the barrels, firing like fury at the enemy in the dim moonlight. He became a killing machine, firing, reloading, and firing again. Mort fumbled and reloaded his own rifle, handing it to Fargo as he rose again to fire, picking off Indian after Indian with extraordinary precision.

Mort's horse, trapped in the corral and fired upon by the goddamned Shoshoni, continued to scream in agony, and each unearthly shriek drove Fargo madder with killing desire. The Indians, still hunkered down in the grasses, were returning less and less fire, moving out of his range and sights. The last of the ranch house roof collapsed in a huge shower of red sparks and the flames continued to roar.

It was time to move. Fargo paused a moment and gave a low whistle. It was the biggest risk he'd ever taken, he thought, calling the Ovaro into this gunfight. And he doubted he'd ever forgive himself if the proud and faithful pinto were shot by the merciless warriors lying in wait all around them. But it was the last ace up his sleeve, and he had to play it or die.

Fargo whistled again, not sure that the Ovaro's sharp ears would pick up the sound over the roar of the fire and the big white's agonized shrieks.

Nothing happened for a while. Fargo resumed firing, but wasn't connecting with many of the Indians. He knew they were cooking up a fresh plan of assault when suddenly he heard the pounding of hooves, and the Ovaro galloped alongside the ranch house toward them. Fargo jerked Mort to his feet and grabbed the pinto's mane as the horse flashed by. Mort was dragging alongside as Fargo fought to gain his seat on the moving horse. With a supreme effort Fargo pulled himself on top, dragging Mort Godfrey up with him. Mort struggled with his one good arm to get a grip around the horse's neck.

There was silence from the attacking Indians as if, for a moment, they could not believe what they were seeing. The strong Ovaro galloped under the weight of the two men, and the corral flashed by them. Mort's big white lay in the center, its haunches blood-darkened, its proud head lifted upward in the moonlight, the terrible death cry of horses in its throat. Fargo took careful aim and fired. The horse's head nodded as if in thanks and then dropped slowly to the earth.

A howl went up from the attacking Indians as the Ovaro galloped toward their line, and Fargo once again poured his fire into them. In another instant they were through the line, and the sound of zinging bullets came from behind them. Fargo hunched low over Mort.

"You still with me?" he shouted.

"Damn right!" Mort shouted back.

Fargo drove the pinto on for another half mile until the sound of gunfire had completely ceased behind them. At the top of a small hillock he reined in. Mort slid down from the pinto.

"Goddamn," he muttered. His shoulder was bleeding, and his left arm hung limp. But he was alive.

Fargo looked back toward the ranch, a gigantic bonfire throwing light across the meadow. His keen eyes swept the land, looking, searching, seeing nothing moving.

No one was following them. It was hard to believe that Shoshonis would sustain an attack for so long and then not pursue the quarry to get scalps.

"I'm going back there," Fargo said shortly.

"Now?"

"Yep. They won't expect me. And I want to see where the hell they're going and what they look like."

"I'll make for that bluff over there," Mort said, pointing to a high rock a half mile farther on. "At the foot is a stand of pine, and I'll hide out there and wait for you."

Fargo nodded and galloped off at a diagonal, toward the high rocks at the entrance to the canyon. He kept his eyes open, but saw no one coming in his direction. Nevertheless, he realized, he shouldn't get too close.

The pinto cantered close to the bluff in the thick, dry grass, staying hidden in the shadow of the high rocks. Ahead Fargo heard noises. He slowed the pinto to a silent walk. They moved forward, Fargo scarcely having to direct the pinto as it edged cautiously toward the sounds. He dismounted and crept silently around a tower of red rocks and peered out toward the passageway entrance to Mort Godfrey's canyon ranch.

The Shoshoni had collected their dead, which were thrown over the horses. Warriors led the packed horses into the narrow passageway. Below them, the ranch house burned red. Fargo suddenly noticed that each of the tribesmen wore the full headdress of a chief, something Fargo had never seen before. And it constituted a fortune in eagle feathers.

The dark figures of the Indians were silent, sullen in defeat. One of the men leading a horse, on which were flung two dead bodies, paused to wipe his brow and wait for a second man to catch up to him. The first man removed his feather headdress and hung it on the saddle horn.

Fargo stared. The horse was saddled. Indians rode bareback.

"Bastards," the first man spoke under his breath as the second one came upon him. "We don't get paid enough for this kind of shit."

The words were clear in the night air. The two men with the loaded horse moved on into the passage. Fargo stood watching the last of the men disappear.

They were all white men, Fargo thought. Every damned one of them. But who the hell was leading them? There was only one way to find out.

Fargo remounted and waited a few minutes. Then

he very slowly rode into the high, narrow passageway between the towering bluffs. There was not a sound. He doubted the men were watching their tail since they would not suspect that he was in any condition to follow them.

He emerged cautiously from between the bluffs and sighted the line of horses moving swiftly now on the far side of the wide flat. Fargo put the Ovaro into high lope and followed, watching as the figures disappeared into the deep shadow between two hills. He angled across the expanse to take advantage of some rough, low ridges for camouflage.

He was hardly invisible, he realized, and if one of the men had stopped to look behind them carefully, he would be spotted. As he approached the shadow between the hills, his sharp eyes detected nothing. The pinto raised its head and snuffed the night wind, then loped on. Usually the horse would balk or snort if it smelled someone waiting. He rode into the darker passage, shielded from the lowering moon by the stark high hills.

After another mile the land rose beneath him, and low rangy pines clung to the hillsides. Fargo dismounted once to check the trail in the dimness and then remounted and continued tracking them. The pinto suddenly gave a soft snort. The clear night breeze brought the faint whiff of a camp fire to his nostrils. At the edge of a stand of pines, Fargo reined in and looked down on a natural clearing below.

The moon had sunk below the mountains. Only faint starlight and the yellow circles of three camp fires lit the scene. Below him was a camp. He counted three dozen tents and a corral with about six dozen ponies—it was hard to make an exact count in the dim light.

So, about sixty men, he calculated. Fewer, since he and Godfrey had taken out a dozen of them that night at least—and wounded others.

The natural clearing was overshadowed by a huge precipice that loomed like a gigantic stern face looking down. A meandering stream glinted with starlight.

Fargo sat watching. He could just make out the moving figures of men piling the dead bodies in a heap far away from the fires. Probably for burial the next day. But if he wanted to know who had hired the men, Fargo realized he'd have to get in closer.

Fargo dismounted and made his way down the hillside. His keen eyes searched for any lookouts, but he saw no one keeping watch. It was hard to believe they would be so cocksure. He lay flat out behind a stand of rabbitbrush and peered out.

Around the near camp fire men were cleaning and reloading their rifles, unsaddling their horses, bandaging wounds, and preparing for sleep. Many of them had already gone into the tents. Conversation was minimal, and Fargo wondered if he would learn anything. Just then he heard hoofbeats coming. Many men, mounted. He shrank back and watched as a group of horsed men rode into camp.

In the lead was Marshal Pike.

Fargo caught his breath when he recognized the tall burly figure of the marshal. He suspected all along the marshal was mixed up in this, but now he knew for certain. Fargo felt his hand instinctively tighten around the butt of his Colt, but he told himself that one lone man could do nothing against such a band. Not at the moment anyway.

"Did you get the Godfrey ranch cleaned out?" Pike asked the men.

"Yeah, we burned him. But there was two of 'em inside. They fought like hell and got away. We lost fifteen men. Ten more shot up."

Pike swore angrily. "Did you get all the dead bodies? And leave a headdress behind?"

The man answered affirmatively.

"Who the hell was helping Mort Godfrey? Who was the second man?" Pike puzzled aloud, a world of suspicion in his words. "I thought we killed his partner already. That kid . . . "

"Don't know who it was, Marshal, but he was a damned good shot."

Marshal Pike paced up and down near the fire for a few minutes, probably puzzling over who the second man was at the Godfrey ranch. Pike wasn't stupid. He'd be wondering if the man he knew as the Butcher had survived the shooting in the river, only to show up at Mort's.

But why was the marshal behind the fake Shoshoni attacks? The attackers didn't steal cattle. All they did was scare the ranchers off their land. That was probably what Pike was after. But why?

Fargo felt his trigger finger twitch again. He could so easily draw and bring down the marshal in one shot. But he knew the marshal's men would be after him, and this time he wouldn't get away. No, the marshal would live until morning. This time, Fargo told himself as he watched the tall figure of the marshal. Yes, he would move very slowly against this man. Pike was a formidable enemy.

With this thought in mind, Fargo silently retraced his steps and found the waiting pinto. All the way back to Godfrey's ranch, Fargo plotted and planned. As soon as he got the ranchers rallied around to run in Marshal Pike once and for all, then he would ride to Cheyenne and meet Lillian Kempner's stagecoach. He hoped he wouldn't be too late.

Mort was waiting in the shadows of the dark junipers. He stood as Fargo galloped up. The sky was already light in the east, dawn's rosy clouds trailing across the sky.

"I was just starting to think I'd seen the last of you," Mort said, relief in his voice.

"They're not Shoshoni," Fargo said shortly. "They're hired by Marshal Pike."

Mort whistled low.

"So, it is Pike after all."

"I tracked 'em over to a secluded bowl overhung by a big-faced rock."

"Yeah, I know the spot you mean. The Smith Ranch used to be over there before they gave up and moved on."

"Well, now it's an armed camp." Fargo felt the exhaustion suddenly assail him. "How's your shoulder?"

The rancher had stanched the blood effectively. Fargo stripped away the shirt and had a look. Luckily the bullet had passed right though, missing bone, but tearing muscle and skin. Fargo took some of the extra bandages from Doc Blair and bound up the wound.

Then they had swigs of water and some pemmican. Fargo let the Ovaro roam, tossed the extra blanket to Mort, and rolled himself in the bedroll. As the sun rose, he fell into a deep sleep, the smell of the smoldering ranch still in his nostrils.

It was just after noon when Fargo awoke again. Mort was still asleep. Fargo quickly laid a smokeless fire and made a hot breakfast of biscuits, bacon, and coffee. The cooking smells woke Mort, and he stretched then rolled over with a groan.

"Those bastards," Godfrey said, sitting up and looking across the wide land toward the trail of smoke rising into the pale blue sky.

While they ate, stretching in the sun, Fargo told Mort all he had seen and heard the night before.

"So, what do we do now?" Mort asked. "There are sixty—well, forty-five—of them and about thirty of us ranchers hereabouts."

"We trap them in their own game," Fargo said. "Since they fight at night, they're bound to sleep in the mornings. Tomorrow morning we're going in."

Mort and Fargo spent the rest of the day resting up. Fargo ran down a mustang from Mort's corral that ran free in the canyon. In the late afternoon they returned to the ranch. The sharp odor of charred wood hung heavy about the place. The ranch house was a still-smoking mass of tumbled timbers. The pot-bellied wood stove, with its long stovepipe pointing skyward, stood virtually undisturbed amid the wreckage.

Mort walked slowly about, kicking at the smoldering logs, leaning down to pick up a charred tin cup and tossing it back into the debris. Then Mort headed for the corral. Fargo ducked inside the shed and found what he was looking for—oats. He brought out the bag and dumped it into the feeding trough for the pinto. Mort stood looking into the corral silently, mourning his dead white. He spent the rest of the afternoon carrying rocks with his one good arm back and forth to build a cairn over the dead animal. When Fargo tried to help, Mort waved him away.

By sunset they were ready to ride. They set off in the gathering dusk. At each ranch, Fargo waited some distance away as Mort galloped in to tell the owner that he had found someone—he didn't say just who—to help them. Then he told each rancher where to meet them. Fargo thought it better to explain everything when all were assembled. By midnight they had passed the word to a dozen ranchers who would fan out and round up the rest.

"Let's get another nap," Mort said tiredly as they left the last ranch. His shoulder wound was bothering him.

There was nothing better to do for the next few hours. They galloped back across the low foothills and toward the shadow passage between the bleak hills. To one side was a low cliff, shaggy with brush. Fargo headed for it. They bedded down there and slept a few more hours.

Fargo awoke an hour before dawn, feeling more refreshed than he had for days. The bullet wound in his thigh, while it still gave him trouble, was better. At last his luck was turning. With thirty angry ranchers firing down on forty-five sleepy and dispirited men, they were bound to prevail.

It was barely light when Fargo and Mort galloped toward the shadowy pass. About thirty ranchers were assembled there, mounted and bristling with rifles. Several of the men started as Fargo rode up, and they recognized him. One lifted his rifle.

"Well, well," the man said, covering Fargo. "If it's not the Butcher of Bentwood himself. After you stole our money, you murdered that poor dove over at the Dusty Rose."

"What do you say we string him up and collect the reward?" another suggested loudly.

"Now wait a minute," Mort shouted over the hubbub as the mounted ranchers pressed in about them, their rifles raised and anger on every face. "Let me speak!"

The men settled down, but kept Fargo in their sights.

"Last night my ranch was burned out," Mort said. "And Fargo saved my life. He's come back here to help us. After we got away, Fargo followed them and . . . they're not Shoshoni! We're being run out by a bunch of men hired by Marshal Pike!"

There was a long silence as the men pondered this. Several muttered in disbelief. Fargo sat silently on the Ovaro.

"What about the dead girl?" somebody else shouted.

Mort started to answer, but Fargo held up his hand. If this was going to succeed, they would have to trust him.

"Hannah Kempner was Mort's partner's girl," Fargo said. "You all know that. After he was killed, she found out something about all this. And somebody wanted her dead. Bad enough to make it look like I'd done it."

"Marshal Pike," one of the men muttered. "It's gotta be."

"Maybe, maybe not," Fargo said. "All I know is he's been after me for a crime I never committed. And last night I saw him leading the men who have been attacking your ranches."

"Let's get 'em!" someone shouted.

Fargo explained his plan to the men, and in the near darkness of predawn they moved out quietly in a double column. Fargo scouted ahead, leading the way through the pass and upward into the rising hills. Finally he approached the last rise, and the top of the stern-faced precipice came into view. Below would be the camp of sleeping men.

The pinto picked its silent way up the incline as the valley below came into view.

It was empty. Marshal Pike and his men had gone.

6

Fargo stared down at the deserted meadow which, the day before, had been an armed camp. Now there was only the silence of dawn and the towering rock face staring down into the empty valley below.

Behind him came Mort Godfrey. He reined in and looked down, confusion on his face.

"They *were* camped here," Fargo said. Fargo's keen eyes scoured the valley and the surrounding hillsides, but nothing was moving. Was it a trap? Or maybe Pike had gotten word that the ranchers were assembling and moved his men. Or maybe they had just left.

"Goddamn it," Fargo muttered.

The ranchers came up behind them silently and stopped to look down at the vacant meadow.

"I say he's lying about everything," one said. "I say we get it over with and hang the Butcher now. The reward on him will pay us back what he owes us."

"But it won't stop your ranches from being attacked," Fargo said. "And if you don't believe me now, let's ride down and look at their camp."

The ranchers grudgingly agreed, and they galloped down the hillside. But, Fargo noticed, several of them now held their rifles at the ready—ready for him, he knew.

At the bottom the grassy land stretched out before them. Fargo led them to the fire pit, blackened and strewn with fresh refuse. He dismounted and looked about while the others watched. He kicked aside the empty food tins and bones that the band had left behind. He knelt over the camp fire, put his hand to the cold ground, and then inhaled. The fire was a day old. Pike had probably let just hours after Fargo had spied on the camp.

"So?" one said after a moment. "This just proves that somebody camped here. If it was Marshal Pike's men, so what? We knew they were around hunting the Shoshoni."

Fargo continued searching, his eyes darting among the grasses. Slowly he walked the length of the camp and found nothing that would tell anybody what the men's real business had been. He turned back for a second look and then he saw it, poking out of a ruffle of yellow grass where it had fallen.

Fargo stooped and retrieved it, holding it high for all to see—a Shoshoni headdress, its eagle feathers dispirited and limp.

"Now why the hell would Pike's men cart this thing around," he asked them, "unless they wore it as a disguise?"

"That's crazy," one man shot back. "Maybe it was just a souvenir."

Fargo shrugged. "Believe what you want," he said. "But there are more of these headdresses in their saddlebags. And buckskins, too. I saw white men dressed as Indians. And I saw Pike ride into their camp last night."

Not far from the camp, Fargo found something else—fresh graves.

"If you've got the stomach, dig up these bodies. They'll be dressed as Shoshoni."

The ranchers stirred uneasily. Fargo sat in thought for a long moment, looking across the empty meadow as the dawn lit the sky pale yellow. The first rays of sun slid down over the stern-faced rock that towered above them.

Wherever Marshal Pike and his men had gone, Fargo did not have the time now to track them down. On Saturday Lillian Kempner would arrive in Cheyenne on the stagecoach. And whoever was behind Hannah's murder at the Dusty Rose would probably be there to meet her. Fargo's thoughts went again to Paul Yancey, the rich newspaper publisher Doc Blair had told him about. Could Yancey be behind all this?

"I've got to get to Cheyenne," Fargo began. "I've got business there that won't wait. But I'll be back."

"Oh, sure," one of the ranchers cut in.

"Look," Mort Godfrey interrupted. "We all know Skye Fargo's reputation. We knew it when we hired him. Now, if he says he's gonna make good, then he will."

Some of the men nodded, and others looked as though they still didn't trust him. Well, that couldn't be helped.

"Besides," Mort said, "I'm going to Cheyenne

along with Fargo. I'll keep an eye on him and make sure he returns to finish this job."

"Let's get going," Fargo said. The sun was up over the hills to the east and flooding the valley with light. Fargo and Mort galloped across the valley. For a few miles they followed the cold track of Marshal Pike and his men.

On the other side of the pine-covered hills, they descended onto the wide plain of white sage and greasewood. Here the trail of Pike's men headed northward.

"They must have gone back to Bentwood," Fargo guessed. Ahead of them, the vast land of the high plain lay under the morning sun. Far in the distance a herd of buffalo darkened the plain as if an ink bottle had been overturned. The riders turned southward and galloped mile after mile throughout the day, stopping at the streams to refresh the horses. The autumn sun was hot, but a cool wind blew at their backs. In the bottomlands, grazing mule deer lifted their long necks and bounded into the brush as they sped past. The hoofbeats of their horses drove the prairie dogs scurrying into their burrows and flocks of orioles fluttering into the sky.

Here and there they saw board shacks and settlements. As they rode through the small town of Hancock, a handful of tottering shacks and corrals, a fluttering white paper tacked to a fence attracted Fargo's gaze. It was a wanted poster for the Butcher of Bentwood. Mort spotted it, too. As they galloped down the street, four horsemen came trotting from the other direction. Fargo put his head down to partially hide his face, but the men didn't seem to notice them.

As soon they were through the town, they turned off the trail and bushwhacked through the rough country. When the sun lowered, Fargo found a site protected by a low cutbank beside a brook. On its banks a few shoots of green still showed among the yellow autumn grass.

"Looks like a good spot," Fargo said, eyeing the cool spring seeping from the rocks.

As Mort gathered wood, Fargo borrowed his shaving kit and soaped up. He looked at himself in the flat disc of polished metal that Mort used as a shaving mirror. Hell, he'd always liked himself in a beard. But, then again, he'd always liked being alive, too. And if those wanted posters had made it to the town of Hancock, then they were certainly hanging in Cheyenne. And anyone who recognized him as the Butcher would shoot first and collect his reward later. No questions asked.

Fargo shaved slowly, taking off his beard but leaving his dark mustache. Then he splashed the cold mountain spring water across his face and looked at himself in the mirror. He looked a lot different. Not to mention that his skin was pale on his jawline where the beard had been. Well, a day or two in the sun would take care of that.

Fargo bagged four rabbits. They roasted the meat on long sticks over the camp fire, ate quickly, and slept well.

They were on the trail again before dawn, the miles of prairie flying by under the hooves of the pinto and the mustang. On the second day the land rose under them as they climbed between the Medicine Bow and

Laramie Mountains ranges. The green ash had turned golden, and drying wild plums still hung on the branches. By nightfall they were high in the Laramie Mountains where they camped in a shallow canyon shaggy with scrub oak.

On Friday, in the late afternoon, they were descending into the town of Cheyenne. The purple shadows lay long before them. Fargo felt rested and rejuvenated. It had been a long ride, but he had had time to think through all the events of the preceding days— the murder at the Dusty Rose and the fake Shoshoni attacks at Windy Gap. He felt more and more certain that Paul Yancey was connected.

As they rode down a long slope, Fargo felt the wind blow against his bare cheeks. The pale skin where his beard had been burned red in the sharp sun on the trail and was already starting to tan. It was a lot of trouble to shave every morning, he thought as he stroked his chin. The day he could clear up this Butcher business, he'd let it go back to stubble. He looked different without the beard, but of course that was no guarantee he wouldn't be recognized. He'd get some fancy clothes that would help disguise him. He'd already decided they'd pose as gambling men.

The town of Cheyenne—five streets crisscrossing a motley collection of board, brick, and adobe—lay just ahead. As they rode down the dusty, rut-dug street, they looked about at the clutter of signs and people. Women in colorful plaid dresses swept along the boarded sidewalks; a group of sheepherders stood eyeing a big ram being auctioned; an old man hawked a wagon load of horse collars; and a cowhand crashed out of bat-wing doors and staggered to his horse.

Just ahead lay the fancy district, a group of substantial redbrick buildings that constituted the entertainment, drinking, and sporting life of the town. On the largest building was a sign: THE GOLDEN HOTEL. Fargo and Mort headed toward a stable nearby where they boarded their mounts, and then they went inside the hotel. The bustling lobby was grand with colorful carpets and oak paneling.

"Even shaved, I don't want to flash my mug around," Fargo said uneasily.

They spotted a newspaper vendor standing beside the grand wooden staircase. The grizzled old man scarcely looked at Fargo as he bought a copy of the day's *Cheyenne Gazette*. Fargo opened it up and slouched against the wall, using the newspaper to shield his face.

"Perfect," Mort whispered. "I'll get us a room."

Fargo scanned the newspaper idly, waiting for Mort to return. An item caught his eye, and he smiled to himself.

BUTCHER OF BENTWOOD GUNNED DOWN BY MARSHAL PIKE, read the headline. The account told how the marshal had tracked the infamous murderer and caught up with him in the North Platte River. The article ended with a quote from the publisher, Paul Yancey, commending Pike's bravery and expertise.

Fargo chuckled to himself. Obviously, if Pike and Yancey were putting about the story that he was dead, it was going to give them a helluva shock for him to show up again. On the other hand, Pike had looked very disturbed at the news that Mort Godfrey had had somebody with him the night of the attack. Pike was not a stupid man, and he would naturally suspect that the Butcher might have escaped downriver and made his way to the ranch. Fargo couldn't trust they wouldn't still be looking for him.

Fargo skimmed through the rest of the paper, and then his eye fell on another article, emblazoned across the top of an inside page: YANCEY TO SEND AMMUNITION TO BELEAGUERED RANCHERS AT WINDY GAP. GENEROUS PUBLISHER MAKES PHILANTHROPIC GESTURE TO SETTLERS BESET BY INDIANS.

Now that was interesting, Fargo thought. The article told all about how the kindhearted newspaper publisher was upset by the Indian attacks. Yancey had decided to send a wagon train of ammunition to the ranchers to help in their fight against the Shoshoni. The publisher was seeking someone to lead the wagon train, and the name of Skye Fargo had been put forward as the best candidate. And, although he'd been seen recently in the area, no one could find him.

Fargo blinked his eyes and read the article again. What could it possibly mean? Yancey was looking for him openly by name, while his man, Marshal Pike, had been hunting him as the Butcher of Bentwood. What was going on here?

Just then there was a stir at the front door. Fargo lowered the newspaper an inch and looked over the top of it. A group of well-dressed dandies had just entered the hotel lobby. Standing in the center of the group and dressed in a fine gray suit crossed in front by a gleaming gold watch chain stood a short man with gray hair and a mustache. His dark sharp eyes took in the room. Fargo knew in an instant that the man was Paul Yancey—rich, powerful, and dangerous.

Yancey continued to examine the lobby. Then he suddenly looked straight at Fargo and began walking toward him, followed by his entourage. Fargo raised the newspaper slowly to cover his eyes again and shrank against the wall.

Great, Fargo thought, as he hid behind the paper. Here he was trying to be inconspicuous, and Paul Yancey spotted him right away. His Colt was in his holster, but he didn't relish a shooting match with dandies in the middle of a crowded hotel lobby.

"Hello, my good man," Yancey's voice said.

Fargo pretended not to have heard.

"Hello, Mr. Yancey, sir," the old newspaper vendor standing beside him answered. Fargo realized that Yancey hadn't spotted him after all, but had been heading toward the old man. He relaxed.

"And how is my newspaper selling today?" Yancey asked. The voice was smooth as a fine cigar.

"Just fine, sir."

There was a silence. Fargo felt Yancey's cold gaze on him, but he didn't lower the newspaper.

"Why there's one of the faithful readers right now," Yancey said in a loud voice. "Let's find out how he's enjoying our publication."

Fargo continued to ignore him. Yancey cleared his throat.

"Excuse me, stranger," Yancey said.

"Don't bother me when I'm reading," Fargo said in a gruff voice.

A few of the dandies tittered.

"I happen to be the publisher of that paper you're reading," Yancey went on. He was clearly expecting that to impress Fargo.

"I don't care who the hell you are. Don't bother me when I'm reading."

There was a shocked silence. Fargo grinned behind the newspaper as the silence lengthened. Clearly, everyone in Cheyenne was cowed by the power of Paul Yancey.

"Obviously, your paper is totally engrossing, Mr. Yancey," one of the dandies piped in.

Yancey cleared his throat, and Fargo heard them moving away. They ascended the grand staircase in a group. Fargo lowered the paper so he could watch them between a tiny slit under his hat brim. Yancey looked out over the lobby as he climbed the steps, his gaze coming to rest again on Fargo. Yancey noticed that Fargo was watching him, even though Fargo was careful not to reveal his face. Yancey stopped and stared back at him. The gaze was full of malevolence and . . . curiosity. And even though Yancey hadn't seen his face, he'd be on the lookout for him.

Yancey and his group disappeared upstairs just as Mort Godfrey returned.

"Got us a room," he said, dangling the key.

Once in the room, Fargo had a hot bath sent up while Mort hurried off to buy fancy duds for them both. The less they looked like they had just come in from the trail, the better.

Fargo lay back, soaking in the warm water, eyes closed. Suddenly he became aware of men's voices, indistinct but fully audible.

It was one of those hotels where the walls were made of paper, he thought. One reason he preferred sleeping in the open. On the other hand, a nice hot bath . . .

After toweling off, Fargo examined his bullet wound again. The thigh was healing nicely. He still had a slight limp, and in the mornings the leg was stiff, but it was healing fast and cleanly. He dressed and paced the room, waiting for Mort's return.

The men's voices from the next room continued. Something about them made Fargo suddenly curious. He took a drinking glass from the washstand and positioned the rim against the wall, then placed his ear against the bottom of the glass.

Immediately the rumble became distinct, every word audible. There were two men talking.

"She's the one loose thread," the first voice said. Fargo recognized the smooth voice immediately. It was Yancey. Fargo smiled at his good luck.

"Don't worry, boss," the second voice said. It was high and quavering. Fargo knew he'd heard it before, but he couldn't place it. "I'll take care of her. Easy as killing an ant."

"Well, just see you don't mess up this time. You've gotten it wrong many times before," Yancey said angrily. "One more mistake from you—"

"There won't be any mistake," the quavering voice

protested. "I tell you, it's easy. She's coming in on the stagecoach tomorrow at six o'clock. She's expecting her sister. I'll just say her sister sent me. The girl's just a dumb broad. It'll be like killing an ant. No problem, boss."

"Just see that it gets done right," Yancey snapped. "Now, get out of here before anybody sees you. And stay away from me in public."

"Yes, boss."

Fargo heard the sound of footsteps and the door opening and closing. Then Yancey's footsteps paced the floor a few times, and then he too left the room.

Fargo put down the glass slowly, a wide grin on his face. He was still smiling a few minutes later when Mort walked in, paper-wrapped packages in his arms.

"You aren't going to be grinning when I tell you who I just saw," Mort said. "Paul Yancey is staying in this hotel. I've seen his tintype, and I know his face. I passed him on the staircase."

"I know," Fargo said. "He's staying right next door. And the walls are very thin." Fargo held up the water glass to his ear.

Mort laughed the whole time they were struggling into their fancy clothes. Fargo told him about spotting Yancey in the lobby as well. When they were finally dressed in the fine linen suits, brocade vests, and wide-brimmed, pale hats, Fargo and Mort looked like two rich gamblers. Mort's bad arm, slowly regaining its usefulness, had a new sling of blue silk. They went downstairs to the dining room.

Dinner in the Golden Room meant a feast. Fargo couldn't remember when he had eaten better. They started with orange duck and went on to roast beef. Each plate was surrounded by mounds of potatoes and various edible decorations. Between courses and several bottles of fine red wine, Fargo filled Mort in on what he had overheard. They finished the meal with the chef's recommendation—a tall tower of yellow and white, which disappeared like a sweet cloud on the tongue.

They played their parts to the hilt. After they ate, Fargo drew a pair of dice from his pocket and offered to throw the waiter for the price of the meal, double or nothing. But the waiter nervously refused.

There was no sign of Paul Yancey in the dining room, and Fargo was just as glad. It had been a close call that afternoon in the lobby, and he didn't want to take any additional risks of running into Yancey again.

The faro games were going strong in the back room. Mort and Fargo lingered for a few minutes, long enough to determine that the Golden Hotel was making a lot of money fast. There was a limit to how much they had to play the role of gamblers, Fargo pointed out. So far, Mort had paid for everything, since all of Fargo's money had been taken at the Dusty Rose.

After watching the faro game for a time, they went upstairs. Once in the room, Fargo listened again at the wall of Yancey's room, but heard nothing. The publisher had gone out. They lay down in the two iron beds. Just as he was drifting off to sleep, Fargo rolled over, fighting the suffocating puffiness of the feather mattress. Another reason he preferred to sleep in the open, he thought.

Saturday dawned clear and crisp. Fargo and Mort spent the morning resting and the afternoon walking about Cheyenne. First they located the stagecoach depot, a small building of new yellow lumber. Fargo gazed at it for a long time, trying to imagine how they would spirit away Lillian Kempner out from under the noses of Paul Yancey's man who would come to meet her.

Next to the depot was a warehouse, and two wagons stood in front. Two men unloaded the wagons slowly, piling wooden boxes in front of the warehouse. Huge towers of crates and barrels were stacked beside and in front of the building, rising precariously above the roofline in places. That gave Fargo an idea.

Mort and Fargo spent the later afternoon sampling the various faro layouts in the gaming houses of Cheyenne to pass the time. At five o'clock they walked back toward the depot and positioned themselves between two buildings across the street where they could keep watch on the depot.

In a half hour Fargo sighted a long lanky figure walking down the street. He nudged Mort, who was cleaning the barrel of his pistol on his brocade vest. Mort looked up and followed Fargo's gaze.

"It's him again," Mort said.

"Dogface," Fargo said.

It was the man Fargo remembered from the meeting with the ranchers of Windy Gap. He would recognize that long, narrow and sallow face anywhere. And,

Fargo realized, it was Dogface's quavering voice that Fargo had heard speaking to Yancey. His suspicions were confirmed when he stopped in front of the depot and took a seat on the porch.

"What was it he called himself in Windy Gap?"

"Joe Johnson," Mort said thoughtfully as they watched the long-faced man.

"Probably not his real name," Fargo mused. Then a sudden idea struck him, and he told his plan to Mort.

At six o'clock Mort Godfrey strode across the dusty street, dodging horses and carriages and stray dogs. Fargo, watching, saw Dogface glance at Mort in surprise and then stand and slink back along the depot wall. So, he recognized Godfrey as one of the ranchers.

Godfrey stood idly beside one of the huge stacks of crates, as if waiting. Just then, Fargo spotted the approaching stagecoach. The Concord came on fast, the six-horse team rearing and snorting with impatience to get to stables and rest, since the horses would be replaced by a swing team during the time the coach stopped in Cheyenne.

Dogface had sighted the approaching coach, too, for he moved forward expectantly. Suddenly there was a disturbance by the warehouse, and crates and barrels went tumbling into the street. A woman screamed and fled to safety. Mort, who had just knocked into the pile of crates, jumped in an attempt to get out of the way. Then he bumped awkwardly and heavily into a second tower of them, which crashed out into the street. Some of the crates sprang open, spilling cans and broken jars. A barrel split, and pickles tumbled out in a green waterfall. Traffic came to a dead halt.

The approaching stagecoach reined in and was stuck, unable to move forward through the tumbled barrels and crates, and unable to back up because of the other wagons immediately behind. A crowd began to gather, and some boys dashed forward to gather up pickles.

Fargo hurried toward the stagecoach, leaping over the chaos. "Why, if it isn't Joe Johnson!" he heard Mort's voice boom out. "We were all wondering . . . "

Fargo couldn't hear more, but he knew that behind him Mort Godfrey had seized the dog-faced man's attention, and probably his arm as well, and wasn't going to let go.

Fargo smiled to himself. The bulky body of the stagecoach stood between him and them. And the crowd would also help obscure Johnson's view. Fargo approached the coach and flung open the door.

"Unload here, folks," Fargo announced authoritatively. He peered into the gloom.

There was no question which one she was. Lillian Kempner was as pretty as her dead sister, with the same light freckles and slender neck, but with pale blond hair. Fargo helped an old woman out and stood aside as a dapper young man descended. Then he put his arm out to help Lillian. She stepped down gracefully, her slender form snug in a yellow plaid dress that accentuated her high round breasts and extravagantly curved waistline.

"Your sister, Hannah, sent me to meet you," Fargo said softly to her.

Lillian looked at him, her eyes wide with surprise.

"Is this your bag?"

She nodded, and Fargo grasped a paisley carpetbag from the pile of luggage and guided her into the crowd away from the deport. He wondered how long Mort could keep Joe Johnson occupied. Every second counted.

Fargo spotted a side alley that cut through to the street where the Golden Hotel stood. He ducked into the alley, holding Lillian's arm. Lillian looked about nervously at the deserted passage.

"Where is Hannah?" she asked suspiciously.

Fargo swallowed. This was not going to be easy. But he couldn't very well tell her that her sister had been brutally murdered and that he was being hunted for the crime. Not yet, anyway. He'd have to do it slowly so that she would understand.

"I'm supposed to bring you to the Golden Room," he said, remembering the words on the slip of paper he had found in Hannah's room. The alley came to an end.

"Wait here just a moment," he said to Lillian. It would be prudent to look about for a moment before making a dash for the hotel, he realized. If Johnson had broken away from Mort already and come looking for Lillian, the game would be up. And, even though Yancey didn't know his shaven face, he didn't want to risk running into him.

Fargo scanned the street slowly. A few carriages and wagons moved up and down. A group of well-dressed women gathered around a shop window. A few men lounged on the front porch of a boarding house. Across the street at the Golden Hotel, all was quiet.

Fargo turned back toward the alley and stopped in his tracks.

Lillian Kempner stood reading a poster tacked on the wall. With one hand she held down a corner of it. On her face was a look of terror.

She glanced up at him as he approached, and her eyes widened in dread, fear and recognition. "Help! Help!" she cried. "The Butcher! Help!"

7

Lillian's eyes were white with panic as she backed away from him down the alley. Fargo took a step toward her and seized her arm.

Behind him he heard men shouting and women screaming, brought by Lillian's cries for help. In a moment they would be surrounded.

Fargo grabbed Lillian about the waist and pulled her close, cupping one hand over her mouth. He spoke into her ear, his voice low and calm. "Yes, your sister's dead. I wanted to tell you slower, but now you know. But I didn't kill her."

Lillian struggled in his grasp, and he felt her sobbing.

"I've been hunting down the man who did it. And I know you have the proof against him. If you don't let me help you, they'll kill you, too."

"Let go of her!" a man shouted. Fargo felt his shoulder seized, and he was pulled roughly backward. A crowd of people had gathered. Fargo hoped no one would be sharp enough to recognize the Butcher of Bentwood without his beard. Lillian had, but then she'd been looking at the poster and was already suspicious of him.

A tall man with a heavy mustache held onto Fargo's arm.

"Here now, what's this about?"

"Are you all right?" Fargo said to Lillian, concern in his voice. Even if she believed what he told her, they would have a hard time talking their way out of this.

Lillian looked at him for a long moment. Her face was tear-streaked, her eyes disbelieving, clearly not yet able to take in the news of her sister's death. Lillian's eyes searched his. Her brow furrowed, and then she decided. She glanced at the man who held onto Fargo's arm and smiled weakly.

"You can let go of my fiancé now," she said. Her voice sounded choked. "He just grabbed me from behind. I didn't realize it was him." She forced a fairly convincing giggle while blinking back the tears in her eyes.

The tall man let go of Fargo's arm reluctantly and moved away. The crowd broke up, the matrons clucking their tongues at such unseemly behavior.

Playing the role of a beau, Fargo offered his arm to Lillian formally and picked up her bag. She took his arm, and they lingered in the alley for a moment more. Lillian turned toward the wall and hid her face with her handkerchief while Fargo stood protectively by.

"My poor Hannah," she sobbed. "I knew she was in danger, but this . . . "

"We're close to getting the man who did it," Fargo

115

said. "With your help I think we can nail him. But for now, let's get inside."

Lillian nodded into her handkerchief and then dried her tears. They hurried across the street toward the hotel. Fargo led the way around to the deserted back staircase that ran up the side of the building.

"The man responsible for Hannah's murder is staying at this hotel also," Fargo explained. "I don't want to risk running into him in the lobby."

Lillian nodded and then hesitated at the bottom of the wooden stair. Fargo could see the doubts in her face again. And he could understand why. He was asking her to take a lot on faith.

"What's his name?" she asked, suspicion in her words.

"Paul Yancey."

"Yes, that's the man Hannah was after," she said. Still she hesitated.

"How do I know you're not working for him?"

"You don't," Fargo admitted. He didn't want to linger beside the hotel any longer than necessary. Every moment increased the chance that someone would happen by and see them. He searched his mind for something he could tell her. Then he remembered Harry Joe Kline, the young boy Hannah had planned to marry, Mort's partner.

"You know the name of Mort Godfrey?" Fargo asked.

Lillian smiled and nodded in recognition.

"He's with me. We're working together."

"Then it must be all right," Lillian said. But he heard the fear still in her voice. She wasn't stupid. She was taking a big risk. And she'd just had a big shock. Fargo followed her up the staircase, and they crept down the hall to the hotel room. Fargo unlocked the door and they hurried inside.

"Maybe you'd better sit down and have a good cry," he suggested. He crossed the room and got two glasses and a bottle of whiskey and filled a glass. "This might help."

Lillian shook her head, still mistrustful and uneasy. A moment later, Mort knocked at the door. Fargo let him in.

"You must be Lillian," he said, crossing the room and shaking her hand. "I'm Mort Godfrey. What a terrible tragedy."

Lillian nodded her head, and the tears started coming. Clearly, now that Godfrey had arrived, she believed what Fargo had said and all that had happened. Fargo and Mort stood by the window, looking out for a while until she pulled herself back together. Mort had arranged a second room next door, and he gave her the key, suggesting that she might want to be alone, but she didn't.

Finally she blew her nose and took a swig of the whiskey Fargo had left for her. "I'm better now," she said weakly.

"You've had a shock," Fargo said, his voice low, "but we need to talk and then move fast. There was another man, one of Paul Yancey's, who was supposed to meet your coach. Mort headed him off."

"Thank you both," she said. She smiled at Fargo. "I'm sorry I screamed."

"Probably a wise thing to do given the circumstances," Fargo said with a shrug. "Now, what is this proof that Hannah sent to you?"

Lillian unbuttoned a deep pocket in the side of her full skirt and drew out a small wallet. She opened it, took out a small newspaper clipping, and handed it to Fargo. He read it aloud.

> Top prices for your land. Interested in Windy Gap area. Bring papers. Paid cash. Number 25 Sage Street, Cheyenne.

Fargo puzzled over the advertisement and handed it to Mort.

"I've seen this," Mort said. "It's in the *Gazette* every day. I was thinking of selling out to this guy. Top prices sounds a helluva lot better than Shoshoni attacks, fake or not."

"So, Paul Yancey must be the one buying up the land at Windy Gap," Fargo mused out loud, "since he's paying Marshal Pike to fake those Indian attacks."

Lillian shuddered violently at the name of Pike.

"He's the one Hannah thought was responsible for poor Harry's death," she said.

"Yeah," Fargo said. "We figured that out. "But what did she plan to do with this proof? And why did she ask you to come here?"

"After Harry died, Hannah was beside herself. And angry. So she took up . . . " Lillian paused, blushing deeply.

"At the Dusty Rose," Fargo put in.

"Yes. Everybody said Harry was killed in an Indian attack, but Hannah suspected it was part of a big plot. She thought by doing . . . what she was doing, she could get more information. And sure enough, eventually, one of the men, one of her . . . "

"Clients," Fargo added.

" . . . was Paul Yancey himself. I didn't agree with what Hannah was doing." Lillian paused and swallowed hard. "But I told her that if she ever needed my help, I would come. Then she sent me this clipping and said to meet her here."

Lillian's voice caught in her throat.

"Hannah knew of a man who could help her get Paul Yancey—somebody named Skye Fargo. Do you know him?"

"Yep," Fargo said simply.

Lillian glanced at him and then stared in astonishment as the realization dawned on her. "You're Fargo, aren't you?" she said in delight, sounding relieved for the first time.

The three of them laughed together, breaking the tension and the grief.

"Well, now we're going to make some plans," Fargo said. "The first thing we have to figure out is this . . . "

He held the newspaper clipping and read it once more.

The next morning Fargo, in his Levi's and leather vest, stood waiting with Mort outside the Golden Hotel. Groups of churchgoers passed them, the women dressed in their finery. The doors of saloons up and down the street swung to and fro—drinking didn't stop on Sundays, and neither did commerce in this bustling frontier town.

In a moment Lillian came out of the front door of the hotel. She wore a riding skirt and plaid blouse. Her blond hair, glistening in the morning sun, was caught back in a band.

"I don't think you should come," Fargo said.

"You can't stop me," Lillian repeated. "Hannah was my sister. I have to know what this is all about."

The three of them walked over to the address on Sage Street where they found a small false-fronted office. The shades were pulled down over the window, but a sign read OPEN.

"Go get the sheriff if we don't come out in an hour," Fargo told Mort.

Fargo and Lillian climbed the steps and entered the office. The front room was deserted. A map of Wyoming Territory hung on the wall over a bare table. A few chairs were scattered about, and a spittoon sat in the corner.

Fargo scanned the room and then moved quietly toward the closed door. It opened.

A portly short man came out, adjusting his vest.

"Howdy!" Fargo said in an overly friendly fashion. "I'm Blue Watkins. This is my wife, Ellie." He motioned toward Lillian who ducked her head, playing the part of a rancher's wife. Fargo pumped the short man's hand up and down. "Now who might you be?"

"Name's Smith," the little man said coldly. "What can I do for you, Watkins?"

"Well," Fargo continued warmly, "we read in the papers that you will buy some land if a man has some to sell."

"Possibly," Smith replied, his eyes on Lillian. "Where is this parcel?"

"Why right here," Fargo said. He crossed the room and pointed on the map to the area of Mort Godfrey's ranch at Windy Gap. "I got me a good thousand acres stretching all the way across that valley, mountain to mountain. Fine grazing land."

The short man stared up at where Fargo's finger was indicating, and his face blushed. He nervously adjusted his collar.

"Oh, yes," he said, trying to keep the excitement out of his voice. "Yes, we'd be very interested in that land. Oh, yes."

"So," Fargo said, holding a chair for Lillian as she sat down, "what's the deal? How much you offering?"

"Well, first we need to see the papers," Smith said, pacing back and forth. "Have you filed a land claim?"

"Oh, sure," Fargo said, seating himself beside Lillian and patting her hand. "Did all that, didn't we?"

"And where are the papers?" Smith asked.

"Back at the hotel," Fargo said.

"Well, if you bring them here, we can talk." Smith stood, watching them as if the interview were suddenly at an end.

"Well, before I go fetching, I'd like to know how much money you're offering," Fargo persisted.

"Let me see the papers first," Smith said.

Fargo saw that he wasn't going to get anywhere with Smith. He rose. "Just tell me one thing," Fargo said conspiratorially. "Who's buying up all this land?"

Just then a voice called out from the back room. Smith jumped and tugged nervously on his cuffs.

"We'll see ourselves out," Fargo said.

Smith jumped up and disappeared into the back room, slamming the door behind him. Fargo motioned to Lillian to get up, and they noisily crossed the room, opened the front door, and slammed it. Immediately he heard voices from the back room. Fargo signaled Lillian to remain standing at the front. Then he crossed the room again and listened at the back door.

"It's fantastic!" Smith said loudly. "A big parcel right in the center, which will connect the whole valley."

"Good, good," a cool, smooth voice said. Fargo knew it was Yancey. "We'll be almost done."

Just then Fargo heard footsteps on the front porch. The doorknob turned. Lillian gasped. Fargo took off his hat and held it in his hands as he started toward the door. It swung open.

There stood Dogface.

The tall, narrow-faced man looked just as Fargo remembered. In a flash he remembered it all now. He remembered the dark night and the camp fire meeting with the ranchers. He remembered the thousand dollars the ranchers had given him. And after the meeting was over, the man who called himself Joe Johnson had sidled over to him. He had some evidence that would be helpful, he said as they rode toward the river and his camp. He was a new rancher in the area, Johnson had said. When they had arrived at Johnson's camp, he had offered Fargo a cup of strong coffee with some kind of herb taste. Thirsty, Fargo had swigged a half a cup and then dashed the rest in the fire.

Almost immediately the world had started to spin crazily, the camp fire dancing sideways, and the river running straight up. He had turned, as if in slow motion, and had seen Johnson weaving his way toward him, carrying a piece of paper and smiling. As in a dream, he had taken the piece of paper and tried to read it, but the words danced on the page, and as he held it to the light, he felt an explosion at the base of his skull and stars skidded across the blackness. As he fell, he knew he had been hit bad.

All of it came back in a flash, all the memories. This was the man who had set him up in Bentwood— or at least the one who had knocked him out. And probably taken the ranchers' thousand dollars off him, too.

Fargo kept his face still, betraying nothing. He smiled in a friendly way. Behind the tall figure he could see several other men waiting outside.

"Just came back in for my hat," Fargo said, stepping toward the door.

Dogface's eyes narrowed, and he shot a glance at Lillian. "Who *are* you?" he said suspiciously, on the edge of recognition.

"We just stopped in to see Smith," Fargo said easily. "Come on, honey, let's go." Fargo took Lillian's arm and tried to push by Joe Johnson.

Johnson sprang into action, pushing Fargo backward. Other men pushed in the door, and Lillian cried out. Fargo hit the floor and rolled once, coming to his feet, his Colt in hand. Dogface had grabbed Lillian and held her around the waist. She bit and scratched him, but he didn't seem to notice. The big men who had swarmed in the door stood stock-still.

"Let her go or I'll plug you between the eyes," Fargo said.

"And you'll be missing the back of your head," a smooth voice said. An ominous click echoed in the sudden quiet.

Without looking, Fargo knew that Paul Yancey stood just behind him. He had opened the door to the back room silently, and now he had Fargo at point-blank range. Fargo quickly reviewed his odds. There were at least ten men in the room—all armed. And Lillian was in danger.

"Toss it," Yancey said.

Fargo threw the Colt down into the middle of the floor.

"Get them in the back room," Yancey said, "before anybody else comes in. Close up shop for the day."

They were led into the back room, a large open area filled with crates. One inadequately small and dusty window threw a dull light across the dark room. An oil lamp sat in a pool of golden light on a bare table surrounded by chairs. Smith spotted them entering and nervously gathered up a heap of papers, then fled out the back door.

One of the men, who looked like a gorilla, pushed Lillian down on one of the chairs.

"Hey," Fargo protested.

"Go easy on the girl," Yancey said.

Their hands were quickly tied behind their backs and secured to the chairs.

Paul Yancey paced up and down before them, looking at them, his face cold and calculating. "Thank you, boys," he said when the job was done. "Now who do you think we have here?" He stopped and stared for a long time at Fargo's face. Fargo felt the man's eyes burning into his flesh, and he returned the gaze with just as much venom.

"Um," Yancey said. "Big man. Strong. Lot of grit. Kind of man I'd like to have working for me. Too bad you're wanted for murdering that poor girl in Bentwood."

"Yeah, boss!" Dogface said excitedly. "Yeah, I recognize him now. Only he used to have a beard! He's that loner fellow I found up at Windy Gap and—"

"Shut up, you fool!" Yancey snapped. A question came into his eyes as he looked at Fargo again. "I thought Pike shot you in the river. Or was that some other criminal?"

"Pike's not too bright," Fargo said nonchalantly. "I guess you tried to get two things done at once, didn't you, Yancey? By getting me out of Windy Gap and setting me up at the Dusty Rose, you stopped the ranchers from getting help *and* you did away with Hannah Kempner."

"Smart boy," Yancey said.

"You had to kill Hannah because she found out about this land-buying operation, didn't she?"

"That girl was always too curious for her own good," Yancey said idly. "But I couldn't resist her." He took a few steps and stopped in front of Lillian. He looked down at her for a long moment. Then he raised one hand and slowly stroked the length of Lillian's cheek. "I guess it runs in the Kempner family—too much curiosity and beauty."

Lillian recoiled from Yancey's touch. Fargo struggled against his ropes, wanting to throttle him. But the bonds were tight, damn tight. He thought of the knife in his ankle holster, but he couldn't reach it with ten men watching him.

"So, you got the message from your dear departed sister, and you came running out to Cheyenne."

Lillian refused to look at him, the color rising in her cheeks. Just then a vague shadow fell across the room. Fargo looked up and saw, outlined in silhouette against the dusty window, the figure of a man trying to peer inside the dark room.

"Go find out who that is," Yancey said smoothly. Six of the men moved off toward a door in the rear of the long, dark room. Fargo hoped to hell it wasn't Mort.

"Just one thing I want to know," Fargo said. "Why Windy Gap?"

Yancey considered the question for a long moment before deciding to answer. "It was only a few years ago the survey teams came through here," Yancey said. "How long do you think it will be before there's a railroad all the way across the continent. Five years? Ten?"

Fargo nodded slowly. He'd heard about the plans for the railroad. Yes, someday it would happen.

"There's only one way over the Rockies north of the Santa Fe Trail," Yancey pointed out. "And that's South Pass. And, unless you want to detour a couple hundred miles north, you got to go through Windy Gap first."

"So, your plan is to take over all the land and hold it for ransom when the railroad is built," Fargo stated.

Yancey nodded, a slow smile on his face.

"You stupid ass," Fargo said. "You think the U.S. government is going to let a few land deeds stand in the way of the transcontinental railroad? Why, when they want to, they'll run right over you."

There was a shocked silence as Yancey's men drew in their breaths. Dogface shifted nervously.

Yancey's face was a frozen mask, a tight smile on his lips. He drew back his hand and started to strike Fargo. Fargo braced himself for the blow, but at the last moment Yancey paused.

"No, no," he said almost to himself. "Must not waste my vital energies on such a peon as you. Must find some better way of dealing with you."

Just then the back door opened, and the six men returned. Fargo saw his worst fears confirmed. Two of them held Mort, who was struggling.

"Hey . . . hey, boss," Dogface said. "That's the rancher who held me back when I was supposed to meet Miz—"

"Shut up!" Yancey snapped again. He looked Mort over. Mort returned Yancey's gaze with pure hatred. "Well, now I have all three of you. The question is, what shall I do with you?"

At that, Mort elbowed the man holding him. He lashed out, kicking Yancey in the side, but wasn't close enough to land a hard blow. Lillian screamed. While the men's attention was diverted, Fargo struggled to reach his throwing knife at his ankle, but the ropes were too tight. He rocked the chair side to side until he could come to his feet, half bent over, the chair behind him and tied to his hands.

Mort was swinging wildly, connecting some blows and not others. The men all had their pistols drawn. Fargo straightened out his arms behind him and twisted to the side, bringing the chair around in a high arc that crashed into the head of one of the thugs standing beside him.

The big man dropped heavily to the floor as Fargo swung the chair toward the next nearest man. It hit him broadside, and he crumpled as it splintered into a dozen wooden pieces. Fargo's wrists were still tied together, and he barreled into a third man, knocking him flat.

Mort was locked in combat with a burly bear of a man, and they were fumbling for a pistol between the two of them. Two shots rang out, and the burly man and Mort dropped to the ground and lay still. Dark blood pooled quickly beside the two bodies, which lay one on top of another.

As Fargo swung out again for the fourth man, another shot rang out and a bullet whizzed close by his ear.

"Stop!" Yancey's voice called out. Fargo realized it was no use. The other thugs had him covered now. He was outnumbered and outgunned. Three men moved forward and pushed him onto a chair and tied him again, this time tying his feet as well. Lillian was sobbing with fright, her head down.

"Oh, Skye, Skye," she said.

Yancey glanced at her and looked again at Fargo, a light in his eyes.

"So. *You're* Skye Fargo, aren't you?" Yancey continued to gaze at him penetratingly.

"Hey, boss," Dogface cut in. "He's the Skye Fargo we've been looking for to take these arms to Windy Gap! Remember, boss, I'm the one who found him! I'm the one who found Skye Fargo up at Windy Gap—"

"You idiot!" Yancey raged at Dogface. "You fool! If you had knocked out any ordinary man, none of this would have happened! But you had to set up the Trailsman!" Yancey drew back his hand and slapped the tall, skinny man hard across the face. Dogface cowered and slunk away into a corner.

Paul Yancey took a deep breath and continued, his voice low and cool as if nothing had happened. "I had been looking for you, Mr. Fargo, to lead a wagon train up to Windy Gap. There's been such bad Shoshoni trouble, you know," he added sarcastically. "And I feel it my civic duty to help those poor ranchers any way I can."

"You've helped them so much already," Fargo said.

"Um," Yancey said, ignoring Fargo's tone. "So, I thought what a good gesture it would be to send this wagon train of rifles and bullets. And there'll be one big wagon of gunpowder—one ton of it—right in the middle. Only trouble is, when it gets to Windy Gap, those Shoshoni attack and set fire to that gunpowder. At midnight that whole wagon train is going to blow sky high. What a pity. What a pity.

"Of course," Yancey continued smoothly, "I'll be

riding up to Windy Gap, too. Maybe a few hours behind. And, by the time I arrive, the poor ranchers will have seen the latest attack. I'll give them my condolences. After all, I'll have done more than any ordinary citizen would. I'll rage against those savage Shoshoni. And then I'll offer them good prices for their land. I don't think they'll refuse."

"Why did you want me leading the wagon train?" Fargo asked.

"I wanted the best," Yancey said, "to show the ranchers my deepest concern for their welfare. But now, of course, I have you. And you'll be making the trip. I'm giving you a comfortable berth inside the gunpowder wagon."

Fargo narrowed his eyes. Yes, he would have expected that from Paul Yancey, he thought.

"Just think of it, Fargo," Yancey continued with great glee. "Three days jouncing over the familiar trail to Windy Gap. You can say your last prayers. And then—boom! All gone! How delightful."

"You can't do this," Lillian screamed at Yancey. "I won't let you!"

"Now, my dear," the little man said to her. He stepped close to her and once again stroked her cheek. "You can stay right here with me where it's warm and safe—at least until I decide what to do with you."

Lillian turned her head and bit his hand, sinking her teeth deep into his flesh. Yancey howled and sprang back, anger flashing in his eyes. Fargo laughed.

"Bitch!" Yancey shouted. "Bitch! I gave you a chance, but you wouldn't have it. All right! You'll go with Fargo. And it will be your last ride!"

Yancey held his bleeding hand as he directed his men to pick up Fargo's chair with Fargo in it and carry it out the back door. Outside was a large yard surrounded by a high board fence. Before them stood a tall mountain wagon, enclosed at the top and sides. The doors were open, and the wagon was half full of kegs. The men lifted Fargo in the chair into the wagon. Then they put Lillian, still bound to her chair, beside him.

"I want your trip to be comfortable," Yancey said, watching. "Give them some food and water, boys."

The men brought several canteens and a knapsack and threw them inside the wagon.

"Why don't you untie us, too?" Lillian asked. Fargo could tell by her voice she was deeply frightened.

"Mr. Fargo will untie you after we shut the doors. But he won't find any way out of that wagon," Yancey added with a chuckle. "I want us all to fully appreciate your grand finale. Boom! I won't be far away and, at midnight, I'll be watching."

At Yancey's command, the heavy doors of the wagon were slowly shut. There was complete darkness inside. Fargo heard the sickening sound of a heavy bolt slammed across the doors. With a jerk and a shudder the wagon began to move.

8

The moment the wagon lurched forward, Fargo began working on the ropes that held him. They were tied tight, but he found that by flexing his right wrist, he could gradually work free.

"Skye?" Lillian's voice said in the darkness. "We're going to die, aren't we?"

"Don't count on it," he said. With Mort dead, no one knew where they were. There was no chance for rescue. They would have to find a way to escape from the wagon before it blew up. The ropes were loosening. In another moment he had his hands free.

Fargo bent over and pulled the knife from his ankle holster. He quickly slit the ropes binding his legs and then shook them off. The wagon was swaying and lurching forward as he stumbled in the direction of Lillian. He reached out and his hand touched her shoulder. She cried out in surprise.

"How'd you get free so fast?"

As Fargo groped in the dark for her bound hands, he touched the softness of her breast. Instead of drawing back from him, she pressed against him for an instant. Fargo smiled to himself in the darkness and hastily cut her free.

"Let's see what we've got here," Fargo said, pulling her to her feet. He held her for a moment in the swaying darkness and she clung to him. "Everything will be all right."

"You're so brave," she said. "Don't you ever lose hope?"

"That's all we've got right now."

Fargo groped in the darkness for the large knapsack. He felt inside. The knapsack had been packed for trail use.

"Pemmican and dried fruit," he said, lifting them to his nose for confirmation. "And a water bucket. Hardtack. And flour—not very useful without a fire. Sugar. And . . . "

He took the cork out of the rough pottery jar he held in his hand. "Now, this is good," he said, inhaling the odor of beef tallow.

"What is it?" Lillian asked from the darkness.

"You'll see," Fargo answered.

"I can't *see* anything," she said. Her voice sounded despairing.

Fargo felt for his shirt and slit the hem of it with his knife, then tore the sewn strip from it. He dipped it in the tallow jar, soaking in the fat and then left a tail of it hanging down the side of the jar.

Fargo pulled the tinderbox from his Levi's and struck a spark. It took several tries before the spark landed on the wick and a small flame grew. In a moment Fargo held up the lamp, which threw a dim light over the wagon's interior.

"Let's see what's here," Fargo said. He stood and held the pottery jar high above him. He didn't want to bring the fire too close to the powder kegs stacked in the other half of the wagon. But he needed to find a way out. And for that, he needed light.

Lillian braced herself with one hand against the wall. Fargo handed her the light so he could explore the interior of the wagon fully. What he found was discouraging.

The mountain wagon was made of solid wood, heavy and reinforced in places with metal rivets. There wasn't a loose board anywhere. The kegs of powder stood in stacks. He moved them to search along the inside of the wagon, but he could find no weak spot, no place where, with the aid of his knife, they could ever hope to pry boards loose.

Fargo swore silently and continued searching for another hour. The sputtering of the flame drew his attention, and he stood from where he had been crawling along the floor of the wagon and took the pottery jar from Lillian's hand. Her face was lined with worry. When he looked inside the jar, he saw that an inch of the fat had already burned away.

"We have to save the light," he said.

Fargo knew he would have to keep them busy to keep their minds off their predicament. And he also knew that somehow, some plan would come to his mind. Sometimes, if he just kept busy, the right action would come clear to him.

"At least we have plenty of food and water," he said.

"I'm not hungry," Lillian said, her voice dispirited.

"Then how about a dance?" he suggested. "Only you have to provide the music."

"Are you crazy?"

In answer, Fargo reached out and pulled her toward him. He began to guide her in a slow circle in the cleared spot. Lillian giggled.

"Have you gone mad?"

"Where's the music?" Fargo tickled her.

Lillian laughed and began to hum a popular song as they danced, sometimes stumbling when the wagon swayed. Dancing was one way to keep them both active, he thought. And to keep her spirits up. And, hell, it gave them something else to do in the long hours before the wagon reached Windy Gap.

Her slender waist was a lovely curve beneath his hands. She pressed up against him, and he became aware of her soft breasts and the hard mound of her pubis as they danced closely. He felt himself harden against her as they danced. She felt it, too, and pressed against him. He nibbled on her neck, and she hummed, deep in her throat.

She entwined her fingers in his hair, pulling his mouth back to hers. Fargo drank in her sweetness, his hands exploring the curve of her waistline, the heavy roundness of her breasts. He slid his hand downward to cup her soft rear.

He bent over, touching his lips to her fragrant hair, searching for her mouth, which he found.

Her lips parted, welcoming his tongue as he kissed her deeply. "Oh, Skye," Lillian murmured in the darkness. "I don't want to die."

She pressed against him, all soft curves and fra-

135

grance. With one hand she began unbuttoning her blouse. Fargo slipped his hand inside and felt the silken smoothness of her voluptuous breast, the nipple soft and warm. He kissed down her neck and nuzzled between the soft mounds, taking a nipple into his mouth, flicking his tongue until it hardened.

"Oh, Skye," she moaned. "Yes. Yes. I want you, yes."

The wagon suddenly lurched to one side, and they lost their balance, tumbling onto the wooden floor.

"You all right?" Fargo asked.

A deep kiss was his answer, Lillian's mouth seeking his in the darkness as she struggled out of her blouse. Fargo kissed her breasts and her narrow rib cage, running his hands over her smooth, fragrant bare skin. She moaned and unbuttoned her skirt, pulling it downward, along with her bloomers. Fargo followed, his mouth exploring the gentle curve of her belly downward until he felt the prickle of her fur and smelled the musky odor of her.

She was wet in his mouth, soft and sweet. He nuzzled between her legs as she groaned, yes, yes. He could feel himself ready for her, and he undid his Levi's, then stripped off his shirt. He paused over her for a moment, at her entrance, feeling her warmth with the tip of him.

"Please, please. Yes, Skye."

Then he thrust up into her suddenly as she cried out in ecstasy. Her legs came up behind his back, and he thrust deeper into her, all the way, again and again, opening her legs wide for him to go deeper. She was tight and firm around him. He held her breasts, massaging the nipples.

"Oh, God! Oh, yes!"

He felt the fire rise in him, burning and ready. Her panting increased, and finally she shuddered under him, and he pushed again, deeper and gave himself completely to her, once, twice, again until only this woman under him was all that existed in the world.

"Oh, Skye, darling," she said, her arms holding him close. Fargo rolled over and held her as she nestled beside him, and in the swaying, creaking darkness of the moving wagon, she slept. Fargo lay awake. His thoughts were filled with plans and his fist smashing into the controlled, smooth face of Paul Yancey.

Lillian slept fitfully, tossing and turning. Several times she called her sister's name. And then his. After a few hours she awoke. Fargo removed his arm from underneath her head and stood up.

He tugged on his Levi's and found one of the canteens. Lillian awoke, and he offered her water. She dressed, and they spent the next hour arranging the objects in the wagon. They restacked the gunpowder kegs to give themselves more room in the wagon and set the bucket in the farthest corner for sanitary purposes. Then they placed the chairs against one wall so they wouldn't stumble over them in the dark, gathered up the cut ropes, and coiled them neatly in a stack by the door. Finally they arranged the canteens in a line and unpacked the knapsack again, slowly, reviewing all the contents.

Fargo realized the wagon was going uphill and knew they were ascending the Laramie Mountains.

He estimated that it was nearing evening. His suspicion was confirmed when the wagon abruptly turned and halted.

"They're camping for the night," Fargo said. He put his ear to the side of the wagon and heard voices, but too muffled to make out the words. He suddenly thought that if they made noise, yelled for help, some outsider would hear them, someone not in the wagon train, perhaps.

But Fargo knew it was unlikely a stranger would happen by the moment they called for help. Nevertheless, he realized, his mind was continuing to sort out any possibility for escape.

Fargo and Lillian bedded down, using their clothes and the knapsack under them. Once they had undressed and lay down, Lillian reached for him tentatively, and he made love to her again, slowly and deeply, holding back until she sobbed with passion and opened to him even more deeply than before. They fell into sleep immediately afterward.

When Fargo awoke, he felt Lillian curled beside him. He pulled away from her and stood, stretching in the darkness. A crack of light abruptly swam before his eyes. He peered at it again. Was it really there?

He made his way toward the light, which came from the doors. As he neared and waved his hands before the light, he knew it was real. He knelt down and put his eye to the light. It was impossible to see out, but the light filtered in between the crack. He put his face to it and smelled a tiny whiff of cold fresh air.

Fargo stiffened. He turned his face back toward the interior of the wagon and inhaled. There was no question that the air was stuffy, stale. He hadn't noticed it before. And they had passed only one day inside the enclosed wagon. Fargo had not thought about the worsening air. The seepage of air through the crack was not enough to freshen the atmosphere inside the wagon. When it got worse, they would have to take turns sitting at the crack to get enough breathable air.

He decided not to tell Lillian. There was no need to panic her. And, if he hadn't noticed the stuffiness, maybe she wouldn't. At least for a while.

The wagon started up again, which awoke Lillian. Together they stretched, bathed minimally using water from one of the canteens, then breakfasted on the fruit and hardtack.

Lillian wanted to dance again, but Fargo realized they would have to keep their activities to a minimum to conserve the little air in the wagon. He suggested she sing instead, and she did for several hours. Fargo sat against the wall and thought.

It was a long day. The time dragged and yet, without an idea for escape, it also seemed to fly by. Fargo thought for the hundredth time about what they had at hand that could help them get out of the wagon.

Water. Flour. Food. Sugar. Bits of rope. Two chairs. One knife. Beef tallow. Clothing. None of it added up to escape. He cast his mind again and thought of the one ton of gunpowder.

Yes, he thought as the plan sprang to life in his mind. Yes, that might work. As Lillian continued to sing softly in the darkness, Fargo slowly planned every step. It was a risk—a huge risk—but it was their only chance.

After they ate a little lunch, Fargo noticed the air was appreciably worse. He showed Lillian the crack in the door. Without telling her his concern, he suggested that she breathe in the fresh air coming through the crack.

"Oh, that smells so fresh," Lillian said, inhaling. "I didn't realize . . . " She stopped speaking for a long moment. And Fargo knew that Lillian had just figured out the additional danger they faced. The air was bad, and they were only halfway to Windy Gap.

Fargo spent the afternoon preparing their escape with Lillian's help. First he pried open one of the casks of gunpowder, using his knife and a slat from a chair. He worked in the darkness to preserve their small supply of tallow and diminishing air. When he finished, he felt light-headed from the exertion and realized the bad air was going to his head.

Fargo sat by the crack for a while and inhaled the tiny bit of fresh air that leaked through until his head cleared. Then he suggested Lillian continue sitting there in order to get a good breath.

Fargo carefully lit the pottery jar, which Lillian held. Then Fargo began to work. Using the point of his knife, he slowly packed gunpowder into six places in the cracks around one of the doors, forcing the gray powder deep into the tight crevices in the wooden jamb. He worked slowly and methodically. Finally he stood and checked the supply of tallow. There was little more than an inch left. Not enough to finish the job, he realized.

"Hell," he muttered aloud, snuffing out the light quickly.

"Is . . . everything all right?" Lillian asked, her voice trembling.

"Yeah," Fargo said. "I'll have to do the next part in the dark."

"Can I help?"

"Sure," Fargo said. "Bring the ropes over here and start unraveling one. I need six wicks."

Lillian did as she was told, her hands untangling the ropes in the darkness. She had done well, he thought. She was scared all right, but some women in this situation would have already been hysterical. Men, too, he thought wryly.

Fargo had Lillian stand well away, and he took both chairs and dashed them on the floor, splintering them. Then he and Lillian crawled about on their hands and knees to retrieve the remains. There weren't many pieces the size he needed, so Fargo splintered the larger pieces into smaller ones until he had a stack of small splints.

They hardly noticed when the wagon stopped again for the second night. Fargo was painstakingly jamming the small wooden splints on top of the gunpowder, fitting the tiny bits of wood tight on top of the charge, while threading the wick in. The air was so thick that he could work only for fifteen minutes at a stretch. Then he would take Lillian's place for a few minutes to get some fresh air.

The night passed like a dream of confused images. After the wood was stuffed and the wick threaded, Fargo found the sack of flour. He poured some into the palm of his hand and dribbled a little water over it, stirring it with one finger to make a very thick paste.

This was going to be the tricky part, he thought. It would take a long time, and he needed more light than they had.

They lit the tallow jar one last time, and Lillian held it close as Fargo carefully daubed the paste onto the outside of the gunpowder charges. With luck the paste would dry quickly and help seal the deposits of powder.

If all went well, when the wicks were lit, the contained gunpowder would explode at the six critical points, blowing the door outward. But, if he had calculated wrong, the charges would simply implode, sending a hail of wooden splinters through the wagon and leaving the door intact. And, at worst, if he had put too much gunpowder into the crevices, the explosion would set off a chain reaction and the whole wagon would blow. Still, possible death was better than certain death, he decided.

The tallow lamp sputtered. Fargo blew it out, leaving a little in the bottom of the jar. He would need it later. In the darkness he finished work on the third charge. The daubing was painstaking. He had to be careful not to get the moist flour too near the gunpowder. Too thick, and the paste wouldn't dry in time. Too thin, and it wouldn't hold.

Fargo swore. Lillian's hand stroked his back encouragingly.

"You're doing all you can," she said.

Fargo bent over and kissed her. His head was swimming again, but he turned back to his work. As Lillian sat breathing by the crack, Fargo found the fourth charge by feel and then, slowly, daubed the paste onto the charge.

A couple of hours later he had finished. There was nothing more to do. He took some air for a time and then lay down. Lillian lay down beside him. The air was better on the floor of the wagon, he noticed. He put his arm around Lillian. There were no words necessary as she reached over and squeezed his hand, nestling under his arm.

Fargo awoke groggy and disoriented, wondering where he was. He fought his way through layers of confusion, and then the swaying of the wagon brought him to consciousness. He had no idea how long the wagon had been moving again. Lillian lay on her side, her breathing labored. The air was thick and hot. Fargo was sweating. He shook Lillian, but she did not awaken.

Fargo stood and pulled her up to a sitting position, then dragged her near the crack. His head swam with the exertion. He put Lillian's face near the light and pressed rhythmically on her chest. She inhaled deeply several times.

"Skye," she murmured. "I had such bad dreams. I dreamed I was drowning."

"We're going to be all right," he said. "As soon as I blow these charges, you'll have all the air you need. We'll be all right."

Fargo didn't want to remind her that blowing the door off would not guarantee their escape. Outside were probably a dozen of Yancey's men, all armed.

Fargo took a few drafts of the air and then felt his way over to the charges. His fingertips told him that the flour paste was still very damp. It would be a while still before he could risk lighting the fuses. He just hoped the men dressed as Shoshoni didn't attack before he could try it.

The wagon was climbing a steep grade. Fargo guessed they were ascending toward Windy Gap. The midnight attack could only be several hours away. Fargo and Lillian stretched out on the floor, taking turns breathing through the crevice. Neither was hungry, although they drank from the canteens.

The air was now so bad that it left them gasping. Any exertion made Fargo's head swim. Fargo found himself slipping in and out of consciousness, his thoughts confused.

The wagons were heading up a sharp incline. For a moment Fargo tried to remember why that was important. Then he remembered they were coming on the last stretch to Windy Gap. He shook his head, trying to clear it. Just then the wagon creaked to a stop.

For a moment, in his confusion, Fargo thought they were stopping again for a night's rest. And then he realized. This was the final stop. The wagons were being halted, and the attack would be staged at midnight.

He suddenly came to full consciousness. It was time. Fargo's fingers fumbled as he tried to strike the tinderbox. Twice the spark failed, and then it caught the wick in the last bit of tallow. Fargo put down the jar and tried to rouse Lillian. She was groggy and limp. He picked her up and carried her to the back of the wagon, depositing her near the casks of gunpowder. It was the worst place to be if the whole thing blew, but, on the other hand, they would both die quickly. He was breathless, his head swimming as he made his way back to the sputtering flame. He examined the six charges. The paste was still damp. It might not work, he realized.

Nevertheless, he lit the first fuse. It caught and hissed. Then he quickly lit four others. The golden light danced in front of his eyes as his head swam. Before he could light the last fuse, the tallow flame sputtered and died.

9

Fargo swore at the fuse. He tried to relight it, using the tallow wick against one of the other burning fuses, but the wick wouldn't catch. The fuses were hissing and burning down closer to the gunpowder. There was just a moment left.

He ran toward the back and threw himself down on top of Lillian. Several long seconds passed as he wondered whether he had put too much powder into the crevices.

Then one of the charges blew. The explosion rocked the wagon and showered him with bits of wood. Another exploded, and then two more in quick succession. Fargo waited a moment. There should have been five. He lifted his head cautiously. Light flooded into the wagon from the door, intact but hanging on one of its hinges. Fresh air blew in. Fargo took several deep breaths. He waited another minute and then figured the fifth charge had snuffed out. Fargo advanced cautiously. Yancey's men would have their guns aimed right at him when he emerged. And he was completely unarmed. He swiftly kicked the door, which swung outward, and jumped backward out of the line of fire. There was a silence.

He looked out. The sunset scene dazzled his eyes after three long days in the darkness. Before him were a dozen wagons drawn up close. Yancey had said that the attack would come at midnight. But none of Yancey's men or horses were to be seen.

They were probably camping not far away. Fargo wondered if anyone had heard the explosion and if they would come to investigate. There was no time to lose.

Fargo returned to where Lillian was lying and picked her up in his arms. He carried her out of the wagon and jumped down, looking about. There was still no one. The wagon train had been drawn up in a tight knot on the top of a high bleak hill. Fargo looked down and recognized the darkening land near the shadowy gap. Yes, by putting the wagons at the crest of the hill, Yancey made sure the explosion would be seen by most of the ranchers at Windy Gap. And then Yancey would claim that he had done all he could to help them.

Lillian came to as he held her in his arms. Her face, blue tinted, began to flush pink again as she took gasping breaths of the sweet air.

"Oh . . . oh," she said, her eyes fluttering open. Lillian looked up into his face, and her eyes widened as she realized they were outside the wagon. "Are . . . we alive?"

"For the moment," Fargo said. He kissed her hastily. Suddenly he heard men's voices not far away. He put Lillian on her feet and pulled her toward the wagon.

"I'm sure I heard gunfire," a man's voice said. "From this direction."

"Well, we have instructions not to shoot until it gets dark."

Fargo peered out and, against the golden sunset, he saw two men approaching. They looked about warily, pistols drawn. In another minute they would pass close by.

Fargo whispered into Lillian's ear, and she quickly made her way back around the other side of the wagon. Fargo peered out again and saw the two men approaching.

"Oh! Who are you?" Fargo heard Lillian exclaim.

The two men whirled about at the sound of her voice. She fled. Both immediately dropped the reins of their horses and sprinted after her, holstering their weapons. Fargo sprang after them, catching up to the one who lagged behind. Using his fist, he clubbed him in the back of the head with a blow that dropped him to the ground.

Fargo stooped, retrieved the pistol, and ran after the second man, who hadn't noticed his partner had fallen. The other man had nearly caught up with Lillian. While running, he reached out to catch hold of her skirt flapping behind her. Suddenly he grasped it and stopped her flight. She shrieked.

Fargo barreled forward and hit, knocking them both off their feet. He rolled on top of the man and gave him a swift uppercut that snapped his head back. The man's eyes rolled in his head and he slumped back, unconscious. Fargo helped Lillian to her feet and took the man's pistol.

"You know how to shoot?"

Lillian shook her head no.

"Well, never mind." Fargo tucked the gun into his belt with the other one. They swiftly retraced their steps. Fargo retrieved the two horses. Then he stood looking at the gunpowder wagon for a moment. The blasts, which had blown off hinges, had not damaged the door, although the bolt was broken. Fargo lifted and swung the door back into place. It hung there, slightly off kilter, but unless someone looked closely, they would assume it was still intact. Soon after, they were mounted. The sunset sky was turning from deep red to purple as the darkness gathered. The attack was still hours away.

The two men had come up the back side of the mountain, so Fargo guessed they were camped some distance in that direction. The smell of wood smoke came to his nostrils. Fargo turned his head from side to side and sniffed the air. The camp fires were just over the rise. The sounds of men's voices drifted to his ears. And then he knew that they had been too nervous about the quantity of gunpowder to build their camp fires too nearby. Still, it was odd that they would have left the wagon train so unguarded. Or was it? They would have to move carefully.

A tight stand of juniper loomed nearby in the semi-darkness. Fargo led Lillian there. He told her to wait with the two horses in the dense clump of trees.

Fargo went quickly alone on foot toward the camp. He met no one. As he headed toward the fires, no one seemed to pay him any attention. The gathering gloom made it hard to discern a man's features, unless he was standing right next to the fire. Fargo realized they wouldn't recognize him either. Nevertheless, he pulled his hat down low and walked on until he was standing near a clump of men.

"Hey you," a man called to him. Fargo glanced over, and the man nodded his head. "Yeah, you. Get this saddle cleaned up for the marshal."

Fargo nodded, suppressing a grin, and moved forward. He took a seat on a log and soaped the marshal's saddle, keeping his hat brim down and his face averted from the flickering firelight. Meanwhile the men moved about him, talking and lining up for the evening meal.

Then he heard two familiar voices.

" . . . three-hour shifts," Marshal Pike was saying as he strode toward the fire. "All around this mountain. I want it so heavily guarded a chipmunk couldn't get through."

"That's right," a quavering voice echoed. It was Dogface. Fargo fought the impulse to look up at the two men, but the anger boiled in his veins.

"And our Indian friends will ride up the back trail an hour before midnight. I want a lot of shooting and carrying on. I'll ride down into the valley and alert the ranchers. They'll be heading across the valley by midnight when she blows."

Dogface laughed a high, delighted giggle. It would be a good show, Fargo thought. And if it worked, the ranchers might fall for it. Right before their eyes, they would think they saw Pike's men battling the Shoshoni and Yancey's intended present go up in smoke. Yeah, they would be discouraged. And a lot of them would finally sell out.

Fargo wiped the leather saddle harder as he thought about what he would do. Suddenly he realized someone was approaching. A pair of large snakeskin boots stopped in the dirt before him.

"She's a beaut', ain't she?" Marshal Pike's voice said.

Fargo paused a minute, then nodded his head agreeably, not looking up.

"You just make sure she's soaped up good," he added.

Fargo nodded again, and Pike moved away, giving orders to other men. When he could no longer hear Pike's voice, Fargo moved the saddle aside. He had found out what he needed to know. And that had been a close call with Pike.

The question now was, what could he do alone against fifty of Yancey's men and almost the same number dressed as Shoshoni?

Fargo slipped out of camp and made his way back to Lillian. He gave her his bandanna to wear over her head to hide her long hair. They mounted, and Fargo had her tuck her skirts beneath her. In the darkness her silhouette looked almost like a boy's. Then he led the way down the back side of the hill, along a ridge, heading in the general direction of the other camp. He remembered what Pike had said about the hill being guarded so well.

To the east the three-quarter moon rose below the evening star. The moonlight threw a weird silver shadow across the landscape. They were nearly down when Fargo felt someone near. Intuition told him they were not alone, but there was no one to be seen. Suddenly a gruff voice called out from a clump of sage.

"Where're you going?"

Fargo jumped and drew in a flash, instinctively. Then he holstered as he realized the voice was that of Pike's guard.

"We got orders," Fargo said roughly. He rode alongside Lillian, trying to keep between her and the spot from where the voice had come, in case the moonlight would betray her.

"Hey," the voice protested as they passed by. "Where are you going? You're supposed to stay up on the hill."

"Orders," Fargo snapped again, spurring his mount. Lillian did the same, and they galloped into the sage-choked narrow passage between the hills.

"Will he follow?" she asked, looking back.

"I don't think so," Fargo said.

Fargo led her in a wide circle until they were out of sight of the sentries. Then he doubled back, crossing behind the hillside. The route took them several miles out of their way, but they came out at the wide plain near the shadow gap, not far from Mort Godfrey's canyon ranch.

Fargo thought of the dead rancher, shot during the fistfight in Yancey's office. He remembered how Mort had fought the thug and how they had been fumbling for the gun between them that had discharged twice and killed them both. He could sure use Mort's help now, Fargo thought.

He would have to ride hard and visit as many of the

ranchers as he could, to tell them what was going to happen before it occurred. Then, when the gunpowder blew up, they would believe him. That was his only chance. And as for Pike and Dogface, well, they would probably get away. There was no chance that Fargo could round up enough men to attack them in the few hours remaining before midnight.

Suddenly he saw a movement on the far side of the wide moonlit meadow. A dark moving line broke away from the shadow of a bluff and wavered across the stillness. They were too far away to see clearly. Pike's and Yancey's men were all up on the hillside. And the ones disguised as Shoshoni were camped under the big-faced rock behind the hills.

"Who are they?" Lillian asked nervously.

"I don't know."

Fargo and Lillian moved their mounts back into a tangle of sage. He continued watching as they galloped nearer, and he could pick out the individual figures of mounted men.

All of a sudden, Fargo saw something he did not believe. He rubbed his eyes and looked again, his keen eyes piercing the moonlit scene. There, galloping out in front, was the magnificently graceful black and white pinto—his own Ovaro. And it was riderless.

Fargo thought he was dreaming. He whistled, a low sound that carried far in the still night.

"What's that for?" Lillian asked.

Fargo didn't answer, but watched as the horse answered, neighing loudly and swinging in a diagonal line, heading straight for him. Fargo whistled again, and the Ovaro sped toward him, pulling away from the dark riders coming behind. They swung around to follow the horse.

Fargo recognized the ranchers. All of them had come, their sturdy range rifles in their saddle holsters.

"It's okay," he told Lillian. "Everything's going to be fine."

Fargo rode out to meet them. The pinto reared up in joy and then kicked its heels playfully. Fargo hastily dismounted and swung into the familiar saddle, feeling the strong pinto beneath him. He still felt he was dreaming. How the hell could his horse get from the stable in Cheyenne out to Windy Gap?

The riders galloped up, surrounding him. Mort Godfrey was in the lead.

Fargo laughed in delight.

"You bastard," Fargo said. Mort pulled his horse alongside the pinto, and Fargo clapped him on the arm. "You looked damn dead when you hit that floor."

"Playing possum was the only way I could think to get out of there alive," Mort said apologetically. "Luckily I was covered with the other guy's blood, and they just threw me out back into the wagon. I got our horses and rode like hell to get here. Arrived at noon, and I've been rounding up the boys ever since. We were going to come get you and Lillian out of that gunpowder wagon. I guess now we'll just head up there and attack."

"I've got a better idea," Fargo said.

Two hours later the ranchers rode in a double column along the trail. On their heads they wore Shoshoni headdresses.

The attack on the camp of fake Indians had been a cinch. There hadn't even been a guard. The ranchers had ridden all the way into the camp before the men realized they were not compatriots from Pike's camp. They had given up almost immediately and were now lying on the cold ground, hog-tied—every one of them.

Fargo smiled to himself as he galloped along on the Ovaro with Mort at his side, leading the ranchers toward the bleak hill. Lillian had been taken to one of the ranches to stay the night, out of harm's way. And now Fargo would finally have his revenge—revenge for Hannah's gruesome murder, for his being set up as her killer, for the Shoshoni attacks at Windy Gap, for the thousand dollars of the ranchers' money that Dogface had stolen, for the attempted kidnapping of Lillian, for locking them in the gunpowder wagon . . .

The sentries at the bottom of the hill hailed them and let them pass by in their Shoshoni feathers. Fargo heard the signal—a low owl call—passed across the hillside as the sentries began walking up the hill to join in the battle. When they reached the summit, they saw a large group of men standing with their rifles ready.

Fargo and Mort melted into the band of ranchers so they wouldn't be spotted. The marshal stood in front of his men, waiting.

"Okay," Pike said. "Now, let's go over the plan. Did you load your weapons with the blanks I sent?"

The ranchers muttered yes, several of them hard put to suppress a chuckle at the unexpected turn of events.

"Fine," Pike said. "Now, we have to put on quite a

show. I want shooting going on for at least an hour. That's how long it will take me to alert a few of the ranchers. We need some eyewitnesses. At midnight sharp, put a bonfire under that powder. And after it blows, all you Indians get back into the hills. The rest of you, put bandages on. Make it look like you fought real hard."

The men nodded and moved off toward the knot of wagons at the crown of the hill, in full view of the valley below. Pike prepared to ride off down the hill to fetch the ranchers of Windy Gap.

"Give me five minutes and then start," Pike said. He rode off into the darkness. Fargo noted the direction he went. In a few minutes Pike's men raised their weapons and began firing. The ranchers did likewise, discharging their weapons harmlessly skyward as they rode about the knot of wagons, slowly moving into position to completely surround all of Pike's men. Then, at a signal from Fargo, they moved in.

"Hands up, move it," Fargo shouted. The ranchers took up his cry. Pike's men, assuming they were playing a game, laughed and continued shooting as the ranchers in the headdresses gradually advanced, tightening the circle.

"I said, hands up," Fargo repeated insistently.

One of Pike's men laughed defiantly and shot a blank toward one of the advancing men. The rancher lowered his rifle and fired at the man, catching him in the arm.

Pike's man howled in pain and shock. He grabbed his arm, and then looked at the blood on his hand in disbelief. A surprised moment of silence was broken by pandemonium as Pike's men realized they had been duped. The ranchers winged several of the men trying to break out of the circle, but by and large they surrendered without a fight, knowing it was hopeless.

Fargo recognized Dogface in the melee as he pushed toward the line, attempting to break free. Fargo advanced on him, fury in his eyes. The moonlight struck Fargo's face, and Dogface recognized him.

"You! You!" Dogface turned to look behind him in puzzlement and panic at the gunpowder wagon. "What . . . what?"

Fargo didn't wait for more. He pulled back his arm, aiming for the narrow face, and rammed his fist in a shattering blow. Dogface reeled backward, staggered, and fell forward to his knees.

"Please," he mumbled, crawling forward. "Don't kill me. I . . . only did what the boss said."

"Let me take care of him," Mort said beside him.

"Yep," Fargo said, disgusted. "I'll catch up with the marshal."

Fargo rode off into the darkness, heading downhill. He still wore the feather headdress. Behind him the sounds of gunfire had almost ceased. An occasional shot was heard along with some shouting of the ranchers as they rounded up Pike's men.

Fargo met Marshal Pike halfway down the hill. Pike had turned and was riding hell-bent up the slope back toward the wagons. Even in the dim moonlight Fargo could see that the marshal was in a fury.

"What the hell is going on?" Pike raged when he

caught sight of the feathered figure approaching. "Where's the battle? I hardly heard any shooting!"

"We already won," Fargo said. He removed his headdress and smiled slowly at Pike. The marshal froze in disbelief.

Then he drew, more swiftly then Fargo could have believed possible, but it was too late. Fargo's Colt was already aimed at Pike.

"Give it up, Pike. It's all over."

In answer, the marshal squeezed the trigger, but his horse faltered under him, and the shot went wide. Pike slid off his horse to use it as a shield. Fargo dismounted and knelt, aiming for the marshal's legs exposed beneath his mount. He pulled the trigger, and Pike screamed in agony. The horse reared and bolted. Pike lay on the ground, clutching his leg with one hand. His pistol lay on the ground, just out of reach.

"Give up," Fargo said again, advancing on him. "I know you killed the girl."

"That bitch," the marshal said, his voice tight with pain. "She deserved it. She was going to betray us— Yancey, me, the whole thing."

"It's over now," Fargo said. "Get up."

The marshal rolled to one side as if preparing to stand. Then he suddenly reached for his gun, bringing it around. An instant before the gun fired, Fargo leaped sideways, and the Colt spat fire. Marshal Pike jerked once and lay still in the cool moonlight.

Fargo stood for a long time looking down at the dead man, his anger draining out of him. It was almost silent on the hilltop above, and nearing midnight. Then Fargo saw a flash of light, a fire being lit, and the flames glowing brighter. In another moment a magnificent globe of yellow fire engulfed the top of the hill, spreading upward into a shower of gold and red sparks. A deep boom resounded across the valley and echoed a moment later, thrown back by the high hills. Flames leaped upward and exploded again and again, shooting light into the darkness all around.

Fargo knew that miles to the east, Paul Yancey was standing on a dark hillside, enjoying his victory.

The next morning Paul Yancey and two men rode up from the south to meet the ranchers in the valley at Windy Gap. Above them on the bleak hill loomed the blackened ruin of the wagon train. The grass fire had burned halfway down the slope.

The ranchers, in a tight knot, rode forward to meet Yancey. Fargo and Mort rode in the center, well-hidden from Yancey's gaze. The ranchers reined in when they neared, the two groups of men facing one another.

"Welcome to Windy Gap, Mr. Yancey," one of the ranchers said.

"Why, thank you," Yancey said in his smooth voice. "I was hoping this would be a happy occasion." Yancey injected a note of sadness in his tone. "Today I planned to deliver that ammunition to help you in your struggle against the terrible savages. But instead, the Shoshoni have defeated me."

Yancey looked suitably somber, and the two men with him shook their heads sadly, stealing glances at the charred hillside.

"But, when I saw this terrible devastation, I decided

to try to help in another way," Yancey said. "I'm offering to buy your land at top dollar. You can all go someplace safer."

"Well, that's real generous of you, ain't it, boys?" the rancher said. The others mumbled agreement. Yancey smiled broadly.

"But actually," the rancher continued, "I don't think we'd be interested." A look of puzzlement crossed Yancey's face. "See, we're kind of fond of the place. You might say, we've gotten attached to our own local customs."

At that, the ranchers reached into their saddlebags. Every one of them donned a Shoshoni headdress. Then they moved aside and Fargo and Mort rode forward a few paces.

Yancey's face went stark white, his dark eyes wide in disbelief and terror.

The expression on Paul Yancey's face was one Fargo would never forget.

LOOKING FORWARD!
The following is the opening
section from the next novel in the exciting
Trailsman series from Signet:

**THE TRAILSMAN #146
NEBRASKA NIGHTMARE**

---

*1860 . . . Nebraska Territory,
where fear and lust exploded
in violence and death . . .*

Night was still an hour off when a murky shroud of
thick fog enclosed Skye Fargo within its clammy
grasp. His powerful, buckskin-clad frame tensed ever
so slightly as his keen, lake blue eyes probed the
gloom ahead for sign of the narrow game trail he had
been following for the better part of the afternoon. To
his right gurgled the sluggish Platte River; to his left a
wall of undergrowth loomed as a black mass against
the gray fog.

Fargo's right hand dropped to his Colt and rested on
the butt of the six-shooter, a simple precaution that
might mean the difference between life and death if he
should suddenly come on something or someone inclined to do him harm. There were plenty of hostiles,
bears, and cougars roaming Nebraska Territory, more
than enough to give lone travelers cause of concern,
and he wasn't about to become one of the countless un-

fortunates whose sun-bleached bones littered the various routes westward.

Not for nothing did men call him the Trailsman, a handle he had earned the hard way. Bloodthirsty Indians, ruthless outlaws, savage beasts—they had all tried to claim his life at one time or another, yet time and again he had survived where others would have died because he had learned long ago to live by three simple rules: to never take unnecessary chances, to never take anything for granted, and to never, ever let down his guard.

So, senses primed, Fargo rode on, his eyes always in motion, his ears catching the slightest sounds. The last settlement was two hundred miles behind him while Denver lay hundreds of miles distant. He was in the heart of untamed, unclaimed wilderness, and for five days he hadn't set sight on another living soul.

Not a dozen yards to the south lay the Oregon Trail, used each year by thousands, but Fargo had neither seen nor heard any sign of a wagon train for the past fifty miles.

An odd tapping noise suddenly came on the cool breeze, causing Fargo to rein up and cock his head. It was repeated, a strange clinking noise, as of metal striking metal. Puzzled, he tried to pinpoint the direction from which it came, but the fog and the intervening brush served to distort it, to give the illusion the noise came from several directions at once.

Soon the tapping stopped. Fargo lightly touched his spurs to the flanks of his pinto stallion and pressed on through the cottonwoods and willows lining the riverbank, the trees rearing like vague, outlandish monsters in the misty soup. He wondered if some of the pilgrims had made camp right next to the river and debated whether to join them for the night. While they'd probably pester him with questions about the West, they also might share a few cups of hot coffee and a heaping plate of tasty food, and he could do with some cooking that wasn't his own.

But no glimmer of firelight greeted Fargo. No murmur of voices confirmed his hunch. Whoever was out there was not being obvious about it, which in itself wasn't cause for concern since only a fool advertised his presence in Indian country. Still, Fargo felt uneasy. He tried to convince himself he was acting like a nervous greenhorn and letting the fog get to him, yet he couldn't shake a persistent feeling that danger lurked nearby.

The trees abruptly ended, and Fargo found himself on a knob of bare ground mere feet from the water's edge. Dismounting, he let the Ovaro dip its muzzle into the Platte while he scanned the woodland. When several minutes had gone by and nothing unusual occurred, Fargo stepped into the stirrups and resumed his journey.

Undergrowth hemmed Fargo in again, so close that slender branches snagged his leggings now and then. He had to duck under low tree limbs, and twice he skirted dense thickets. Rather than be relieved by the quiet gripping the prairie, he became certain that he was no longer alone.

Presently the Ovaro nickered and swung its head to

the left, peering intently into the fog. Fargo did likewise, knowing from long experience to rely on the
stallion's sharper hearing and sensitive nostrils. All he
saw was the swirling vapor. Whatever was shadowing
him was keeping its distance.

Moments later the pinto halted of its own accord
and nervously bobbed its head. Fargo urged the horse
onward, but the stallion balked, prompting him to
loosen the Colt in its holster for a quick draw. Then he
noticed that the Ovaro was staring down low, as if at
something close to the ground a dozen feet away. He
squinted and thought he detected an inky shape creeping forward, a four-legged creature by the look of it.

The Colt leaped clear. Fargo had the hammer
cocked and his finger was beginning to tighten on the
trigger when the fog thickened, cutting off his view of
the thing. Impatiently he waited for another glimpse
so he could be sure of his shot, but when the fog
thinned a bit, he was annoyed to discover the silent
stalker had disappeared.

Fargo was fairly certain he had seen a cougar. Although not as numerous on the plains as they were in
the mountains, the big cats had been known at attack
men on occasion and often preyed on livestock.
Horseflesh, in particular, was one of their favorite
meals. Evidently this one was hungry enough to risk
tangling with him to get at the Ovaro, which he must
prevent at all costs. Besides being fond of the pinto,
he was well aware that being stranded afoot in the
middle of nowhere was a sure invitation for trouble.

With nightfall rapidly approaching, the strip of forest was growing darker and darker. It wouldn't be long before the combination of fog and night put Fargo completely at the cougar's mercy. He knew that he had to get out of the trees or find a clearing in which to make a stand.

A faint scratching told Fargo the lion was now to his rear. Shifting in the saddle, he slid the Colt into its holster and shucked his Sharps instead. The heavy-caliber rifle had more stopping power than the pistol; a single shot could drop a bull buffalo or a grown grizzly in its tracks.

Tense seconds elapsed. Fargo prodded the stallion into a brisk walk, unable to go any faster for fear of colliding with a log or some other obstacle. Constantly glancing right and left, he came to a bend in the Platte. Either he bore along the bank to the south or crossed to the other side.

Fargo picked the latter. Most cats shunned water, and cougars were no exception. He was counting on the cougar to give up rather than get wet, so into the river he plunged, the level rising swiftly to just below the soles of his boots. The Platte River flowed in a shallow channel so he need not worry about soaking his few belongings. Angling into the current, he allowed the Ovaro to carefully pick its way.

The crisp snap of a twig brought Fargo around with the rifle at his shoulder. He spied an indistinct form on the bank, at the very spot he had just vacated, and he hastily took a bead. Once more the fog frustrated him, obscuring the hazy outline.

"Damn it," Fargo grumbled, half under his breath.

Lowering the Sharps, he picked up the pace, and he was emerging onto a gravel bar when a loud splash alerted him that the cougar was more persistent than he would have liked.

Fargo moved slowly along the shore, seeking sign of it in the river where picking it off would be as easy as shooting clay targets. He had gone fifteen yards when a figure appeared in front of the stallion, popping out of the mist as if sprouted by the very earth. As quick as he was in snapping the rifle up, the cougar was quicker and instantly vanished into the brush.

The situation had not changed a whit. Sooner or later the lion would tire of the cat-and-mouse hunt and pounce, and Fargo was powerless to do a thing about it. Or was he? Acting on inspiration, Fargo turned the Ovaro back into the river and trotted around the bend, hugging the bank where the water came only to the stallion's ankles. Here there were no obstacles and he could make good time.

A crackling in the woods showed the cougar was trying to parallel the Trailsman's course.

Fargo marveled that the predator was making so much noise. Ordinarily cougars were as silent as ghosts. They had to be in order to bring down game. This one was behaving unlike any other he had ever heard of, which caused him to speculate whether it was aged or infirm or possibly a confirmed man-eater. Some of the old-timers claimed that once a cougar tasted human flesh, it developed a strong hankering for more.

The stallion had covered nearly fifty yards when Fargo spotted something slanting toward him from out of the cottonwoods. This time he was ready. His Sharpe thundered the moment he saw the thing. Too late, he realized the shape was much larger than that of any mountain lion. He heard a frightened whinny— a horse—as it wheeled and galloped away.

Without thinking, Fargo swept out of the river in determined pursuit. He hadn't glimpsed a rider, which made no difference. Since he was responsible, he had to do what he could for the poor animal. Wounded, perhaps in great pain, it was plowing through the undergrowth with no regard for its own welfare, and in so doing was making as much noise as a herd of panicked buffalo. He stayed hard on its heels with ease.

Presently the horse veered to the left, bearing toward the Platte. By the time Fargo reached the bank, the horse was almost to the south side and barely visible. Shoving the Sharps into the boot, he reentered the river. The fog was finally starting to break, but not fast enough to suit him.

Apparently the wounded horse had a destination in mind, for once it attained the south shore it sped due west at a clip that most ordinary mounts would have envied. Fargo wished he could see the ground plainly enough to note whether there were any fresh marks of blood so he could gauge how badly the horse was hurt. He figured it must be an Indian mount, or maybe an animal that had strayed away from a wagon train and become lost. The following moment, all thought of the chase was forgotten as the twilight was shattered by the unexpected shout of a female voice.

"Lancelot!"

Fargo hauled on the reins, bringing the Ovaro to a sliding stop.

"Lancelot! Where the dickens are you?"

Homing in on the cry, Fargo wound through the trees. In light of the sequence of events, he was totally perplexed. What was a woman doing there? And who in the hell was Lancelot? He hadn't gone thirty feet when he saw someone approaching.

"Lancelot?"

There was a glimmer of golden hair. Before Fargo could answer, a loud gasp escaped the woman's lips, and she spun and fled. "Hold on!" he yelled. "I won't do you harm!"

Whoever she was, she paid no heed. Her lithe body sheared through hovering tendrils of lingering fog as she ran, her long skirt billowing about her shapely legs.

"Hold on!" Fargo repeated, going after the woman for her own good. With the cougar still in the vicinity, it wouldn't do to have her stumbling around in the brush. "I just want to talk!" he added, to no avail.

The woman's blond hair served handily as a beacon, enabling Fargo to close the gap rapidly. He was only a few yards to her rear when she suddenly faced around, a small gun blossoming in her right hand.

"Come no closer or I'll shoot!"

They were so close by then that Fargo was almost upon her even as he drew rein. The click of a hammer warned him of his peril a heartbeat before she fired, and in order to avoid being shot he hurled himself to the right, leaving the saddle in a neat dive that carried him into a cluster of high weeds. Rolling to one side, he rose to his knees and elevated his arms to show he had friendly intentions.

"Didn't you hear me, lady?" he demanded. Only she was already gone, flitting to the southwest like a spectral bird.

The Ovaro, meanwhile, had not slowed a hair and was still bearing westward on the trail of the wounded horse.

Fargo rose, then hesitated. Should he go after the stallion or the woman? Scowling, he ran to the southwest, deeper into the woods, bellowing, "Stop, you idiot! There's a lion hereabouts!"

A frightened glance was the woman's sole reaction. Limbs flying, she darted past a willow, tripped over a root, and catapulted head over heels. Her smooth thighs flashed pale in the dusk, and then she was lying on her back.

"Are you all right?" Fargo asked as he caught up and leaned down to offer her his hand. She was a beauty, with flashing green eyes and a creamy complexion. Plus a deadly derringer which she lifted and touched to the tip of Fargo's nose.

"Don't twitch a muscle, mister. I won't miss at this range."

"Yes, ma'am," Fargo said dutifully, resisting an impulse to snatch the parlor gun from her grasp and give her a resounding slap for her ungrateful attitude. "I never argue with a lady as fond of slinging lead as you seem to be."

"Back up. Keep your hands where I can see them."

Sighing, Fargo complied. His gaze lingered on her swelling bosom as she stood and absently brushed her bangs aside with a practiced gesture. "Are you always so friendly? Or aren't you partial to men with beards?"

Her spine stiffening, the blonde regarded him coldly. Or tried to, but a hint of a grin touched the corners of her luscious mouth. "You're right handsome, mister, if that's the compliment you're fishing for. But good looks don't count for much when a girl stands to lose her life if she isn't mighty careful."

"I told you that I meant you no harm," Fargo pointed out.

"And I'm supposed to take your word as gospel?" The woman snorted. "I don't even know you."

Fargo introduced himself.

"The name means nothing to me. For all I know, Rascomb sent you to deal with us. Not that we don't have enough problems with Nightmare and all." She hefted her dainty hardware. "Take out that hog-leg of yours and set it down real nice and slow."

Although Fargo was inclined to do no such thing, he reluctantly obeyed. Women and guns, he had found, were a ticklish proposition, particularly when the woman involved was fidgeting nervously and might accidentally squeeze the trigger if he so much as sneezed.

"You did that nicely," the blonde said with a smirk. "I bet one day you make someone a fine husband."

"I'm not the marrying kind."

"Too bad," the woman said, rather wistfully. Motioning him backward, she carefully bent her knees to retrieve his six-gun. "I'm Samantha Walker, by the way."

"How far off is the wagon train you're with?"

"What gives you the idea I belong to one?"

"Well, you're sure as hell not traipsing around Indian country all by yourself," Fargo said. "And most folks using the Oregon Trail do so in prairie schooners or some other kind of light wagon. So where's the train?"

"Such a know-it-all! For your information I *live* near here."

"And I'm liable to sprout wings and go flapping into the sky any time now."

Hearty laughter burst from Samantha. "My, my. A doubting Thomas! You sound so sincere, I almost believe you."

"I'm not in the habit of lying," Fargo said.

Samantha studied his features before responding. "You do have the look of an honest man, which is more the pity. I want to believe you, mister. I truly do. Back before all this nasty business started I would have taken your word without batting an eye. But three families have already been driven off, and two of the men have been badly beaten. No one dares trust a stranger anymore." Her slender shoulders drooped.

"Between Rascomb and Nightmare we haven't known a moment's peace in pretty near a whole year."

"That's twice you've mentioned those names. Who are they?"

"I'll tell you about them while we walk," Samantha said, wagging the Colt toward the Platte. "And once you know the story, maybe then you won't think so poorly of me."

Fargo didn't bother mentioning that she needn't have worried about his opinion of her. He'd been quite impressed by the confident tilt of her chin and the lively spark in her eyes, to say nothing of the promising contours of her lush body hinted at by the way her clothes clung to her figure. Without protest he hiked toward the river, wisely keeping his arms out from his sides where she could plainly see them.

"We were on our way to the Promised Land when my pa got the idea to settle here instead," Samantha began. "Why go all the way to Oregon, he asked us, when everything we wanted was right here for the taking? There's water galore, what with the river and all, and a person couldn't find sweeter grass or richer soil anywhere."

"Your pa is right about that," Fargo commented when she paused. In fact, he had long expected an enterprising emigrant to get just such an idea since the area bordering the Platte River was as suitable for homesteading as anywhere else west of the Mississippi. Except for one minor stumbling block. "But what about the Indians?"

"The tribes that cause so much grief all live north

of the Platte," Samantha reminded him. "The Pawnees are the closest, but they know better than to molest people using this stretch of the Oregon Trail since the Army can have troops here in short order to deal with them. There hasn't been an Indian attack in this particular area for over ten years now."

"And the Sioux and Cheyenne are well west of here," Fargo said, "so they leave you alone, too."

"That they do," Samantha confirmed. "A hunting party of Sioux out after buffalo did come on us once. They rode right up to our house. My pa had us feed them and give them a few things, and they went away as happy as could be."

"This pa of yours sounds like a smart man," Fargo said. Most settlers would have shot at the Sioux on sight and been wiped out for their stupidity.

"He sure is," Samantha responded proudly. "He was the one who figured out we could buy all the supplies we want from folks taking the Trail. Most of them load up with a lot more stuff than they need for the journey, so they don't object to lightening their loads any."

"Which saves you from having to make a lot of trips to the settlements."

"We haven't gone since we got here," Samantha said. "But Ma has been itching to see her sister so we may go next spring." She paused. "If things quiet down by then."

Fargo was about to press her for details when a feral rumbling erupted from a thicket off to the right, which in turn was punctuated by the blast of his Colt as Samantha Walker took several steps nearer the vegetation and wildly squeezed off a pair of shots. In the ensuing silence there was a ringing in Fargo's ears. "Those are my bullets you're wasting," he chided. "Next time wait until you see something to shoot at. All you did was scare the thing off."

"Gunfire doesn't bother him! He's stalking us!"

"Who is?"

"Nightmare! The cougar that ripped Mr. Aarons apart a few months ago. The same one that's been slaughtering a lot of our stock."

"It must be the lion I saw a while back. I tried to warn you about—"

"We've got to reach the house!" Samantha interrupted excitedly, motioning for him to continue. "My pa will want to sic the dogs on Nightmare while he's still close by. This time they won't lose the scent!"

"Why not let me have my six-gun?" Fargo suggested. "If that cat shows its whiskers, I'll put an end to it right here and now."

"Nothing doing. You just keep walking."

Fargo could no longer afford to humor her, not when the cougar might be circling them at that very moment, girding itself to attack. He pretended to do as she wanted, and half turning, he took a single step. Out of the corner of his eye he saw her glance anxiously at the thicket, which was all the distraction he required. In a twinkling he was at her side, his left hand seizing her wrist as his right tore the Colt from her grasp. She recoiled in fear and tried to bring her derringer to bear, but he already had the barrel of the

Colt pressed to her nose in imitation of what she had done to him minutes before. "Don't do something you'll regret," he cautioned.

Samantha froze.

"If you promise to behave yourself, you can keep your parlor gun," Fargo said.

The offer surprised her. "You'd trust me not to shoot you the minute you turn your back?"

"If you do," Fargo said, "I'm liable to get riled enough to put you over my knee and give you a good spanking."

"I had no idea you were so wicked at heart," Samantha said, trying to sound annoyed, but unable to hide the amusement crinkling the corners of her eyes. "You'd like to do that, wouldn't you?"

"I'm not made of stone." Fargo released her wrist and twirled the Colt into his holster. "And something tells me you'd like it just as much as I would."

"How dare you!" Samantha said, her reproach as fake as the glare she bestowed on him. "I'll have you know I don't throw myself at every handsome ruffian I meet." She opened her mouth to say more when her gaze drifted past him and sheer terror replaced her mock anger. "Look out!" she screamed. "It's Nightmare!"

By the year 2000, 2 out of 3 Americans could be illiterate.

It's true.

Today, 75 million adults...about one American in three, can't read adequately. And by the year 2000, U.S. News & World Report envisions an America with a literacy rate of only 30%.

Before that America comes to be, you can stop it...by joining the fight against illiteracy today.

Call the Coalition for Literacy at toll-free **1-800-228-8813** and volunteer.

Volunteer Against Illiteracy.
The only degree you need is a degree of caring.